Tell Me No Lies

Tell Me No Lies

Linda Hope Lee

Five Star • Waterville, Maine

First Edition
First Printing: January 2006

Published in 2006 in conjunction with Tekno Books.

Set in 11 pt. Plantin.

Printed in the United States on permanent paper.

Library of Congress Cataloging-in-Publication Data

Lee, Linda (Linda Hope)
    Tell me no lies / by Linda Hope Lee.—1st ed.
        p. cm.
    ISBN 1-59414-416-8 (hc : alk. paper)
    1. Painters—Fiction.   2. Seattle (Wash.)—Fiction.   I. Title.
PS3557.O618T45 2006
813'.6—dc22   2005027049

For Ted,
and in memory of our wirehaired fox terrier, Wendy,
fellow travelers on the journey that inspired this story.

Chapter One

"I wish you wouldn't take this job, dear."

Julie Foster turned from loading a suitcase into the back of her canopied, red Ford truck to find her mother's usually placid features twisted into a look of dismay.

She laid a reassuring hand on the older woman's shoulder. "Don't worry, Mom, everything is going to be okay. No one in Cooperville will ever know our secret. To them, I'm just Julie Foster, the artist they commissioned to paint their town's murals. I'll get the job done and be back home before you know it."

Eleanor continued to frown. Julie moved closer and gave her a quick hug. "Come on, Mom, you came over to help me pack."

Eleanor's features relaxed into a sheepish look. "You're right. I did come to help, not to stand around worrying. What goes in next?"

"How about the suitcase by the steps, and then the box of paintbrushes. They shouldn't be too heavy for you. I packed both light."

Earlier, Julie had stacked everything she was taking to Cooperville outside the back entrance to her Seattle apartment. The spot was convenient to her truck, which she kept in the building's covered parking lot.

Eleanor picked up the tan leather suitcase and carried it to the truck. "When will Audra be joining you?" she asked.

Audra DeSoto was an artist friend Julie had hired to help her with the Cooperville murals.

"Not till I'm ready to start painting." Julie reached down to fasten a piece of packing tape that had come loose from one of the boxes. "For the first couple of weeks, I'll be working with the town's Murals Committee to design the murals. They want all three to be historical, so I'll have to do some research. I understand Cooperville has a fabulous museum, and there will be plenty of resources."

"This is a good opportunity for you," Eleanor conceded, as she returned for the box of Julie's paintbrushes. "If only—"

Knowing where her mother was headed, Julie interrupted. "Mom, what happened in Cooperville was a long, long time ago."

"Only a couple of generations ago," Eleanor corrected.

"Still, I'll bet no one even remembers."

"The Linscotts remember." Eleanor nodded emphatically. "And you have to work directly with Millie Linscott. You told me she's the Chairperson of the Murals Committee."

"Right."

"But Millie was Cyrus Linscott's wife. Cyrus owned the Cooperville Bank, where your grandfather Ben worked."

"We've been through this before, Mom. I know what you're going to say next. That Grandpa Ben was accused of embezzling money from the bank."

"Doesn't that make a difference to you?"

"No, because he was never proven to be the thief."

Eleanor put the box of paintbrushes into the back of the truck. "Only because he ran away and never faced a trial."

"Well, he's dead now, rest his soul. Millie Linscott doesn't know I'm his granddaughter. She'll never know. I have a different last name than his. I won't have anything to do with the

8

bank. The murals are to be painted on the library, museum, and theater walls. I promise I won't go near the bank."

"I still don't like the idea of you being in Cooperville," Eleanor persisted.

"I've thought this all through and decided it will work. Please, Mom, support me."

"I do support you, dear. I just don't want you to suffer for what happened to Grandpa Ben. If Millie or any of the other Linscotts should somehow find out your relationship to Ben, you'll be in trouble. The Linscotts never forget—or forgive—a wrong done to them."

"When Millie Linscott interviewed me, she seemed quite nice and reasonable."

"Oh, yes, as long as you don't cross her."

"Mom, you haven't seen Mrs. Linscott since you were a child. How do you know she hasn't changed?"

"She hasn't. Count on it." Eleanor was quiet for several seconds, staring at Julie as though she wanted to say more.

"What?" Julie prompted.

"Oh . . . nothing. I'll just worry till this is all over."

An hour later, Julie left her mother and her apartment behind. Eleanor had promised to water Julie's plants, and Julie had promised to phone home regularly.

Her red truck rolled along, the tires humming on the freeway pavement. She traveled north, then turned east, toward the Cascades Highway, which would take her across the state to Cooperville. She'd drive as far as she could today, stop for the night, and arrive at her destination early tomorrow morning. That would give her the entire day to get settled in the motel where she was to stay and to get ready to meet with the Murals Committee on Saturday.

Designing and painting the Cooperville murals was a wonderful career opportunity for Julie. After studying fine art at the prestigious Dunley Art School, she decided that painting the large wall pictures would be her focus. She luckily gained an apprenticeship with Gerard Bronson, the well-known Northwest muralist. Now, she had a job in which she would be in charge. With all the small towns scattered throughout the Northwest, the possibilities for other assignments were practically endless.

However, she had to admit her mother's worries nagged her. Julie had experienced misgivings when she'd first applied for the Cooperville job, because of Grandpa Ben and his trouble there.

When she'd been offered the project, she hadn't been able to turn it down. She was eager to make a name for herself painting murals, and this opportunity would give her a wonderful start.

She needn't worry. As she had reminded her mother, she didn't carry a last name the Linscotts would recognize. Her last name was Foster, not Gabriel, like Grandpa Benjamin's. Julie's mother had been a Gabriel until she married Julie's father, Tom Horton. Even if someone recognized the name Horton, it was no longer Julie's. After Julie's father died, Eleanor had wed Lowell Foster. Lowell adopted Julie, and she had taken his name.

She was, therefore, far removed from anything that had happened between the Gabriels and the Linscotts.

As for Millie Linscott, Julie was sure her mother was wrong about her. The woman would be no trouble. No trouble at all.

The following morning, at her home in Cooperville, Millie Linscott put down her teacup and gazed over the top of her glasses at her grandson, Gregory, who sat across the table from her. Gregory lived next door to Millie's estate in a small farmhouse he'd recently purchased. A couple of times a week he crossed the stream that separated their properties and joined her for breakfast. Since it was summertime, they ate on the screened porch overlooking Millie's extensive gardens.

Although she saw Gregory frequently, she never failed to be struck by his handsome features. He had the Linscotts' high forehead, chiseled nose, and determined chin, the same masculine good looks that had attracted her to his grandfather, Cyrus, over fifty years ago.

Gregory had inherited her eyes, however. They were the color of melted chocolate and framed with thick lashes. The same brown eyes that Millie knew had charmed Cyrus. Yes, she and Cyrus had been a good match, in so many ways. But he was long dead, rest his dear, sweet soul. And she had been left to carry on the Linscott legacy.

Millie turned her thoughts away from her lost love to the matter currently on her mind, the one she wanted to discuss with Gregory. She said to him, "I wish you weren't so against our murals project."

He glanced up from reading *The Wall Street Journal*, which he had folded small enough to fit beside his plate. He wasn't being rude; she quite approved of his keeping up with the news. But on this particular morning, she wanted to talk.

Gregory sipped his coffee before replying. "Sorry, Gran, but there are so many more important things that could be done with the money."

"I suppose you're referring to your own pet project of a teen center." Gregory had long been interested in helping the town's small, but sometimes volatile, population of troubled teenagers.

"Sure, I want to see a center built. But there are other things, too. For example, if you want to spruce up the town, why not buy new benches and picnic tables for the park? Or plant more trees along the downtown sidewalks?"

Millie sniffed. "The Park Department has a budget, which they fritter away. I don't approve of giving them any more money. And don't forget that much of the murals' costs are being paid for by a state grant and by donations from various businesses."

"Including our bank," he interjected, referring to the Cooperville First National Bank, owned by the Linscotts, and where he worked as loan officer.

"Yes, and since our bank is one of the three buildings to be painted, I hope you'll be cooperative when the time comes."

Gregory sighed. "Of course, I will. But that doesn't mean I have to agree with it."

"We've hired a really talented muralist." Millie picked up a blueberry muffin and split it in half with her knife. She really shouldn't indulge in a second helping, but Hilda's muffins were impossible to resist. Millie could only blame herself for having hired a cook who loved to make pastries.

"She's from Seattle," Millie went on about the artist. "And she'll be staying here for the entire summer. The committee and I figured it would take that long to complete all the murals."

"Mmmm hmmm." Gregory's gaze strayed back to his newspaper.

"The committee is having a reception for her. It's going to be here, on Saturday evening. I hope you'll be available." Millie raised her eyebrows expectantly.

"A command performance, huh?" he said in a teasing tone. "Sure, I'll come."

"Good, I need you. I know we have a large extended family, most of whom are always available to help, but you're the one I count on the most."

Millie sighed. She'd wanted to have several children, but there had been only one before Cyrus died. Winston had been a good son, but, unfortunately, when he grew up he was not interested in the family businesses. A few years after Gregory was born, Winston divorced his wife and ran off to a South Seas Island. There he'd contracted a strange fever and died. Shortly after that, Gregory's mother had passed away from a particularly invasive form of cancer. Millie had raised Gregory.

Fortunately, Gregory had taken after her and Cyrus, and had inherited a level-headedness and a business sense that had made him most suitable to enter the banking business as well as to manage their other family interests. Yes, Gregory was the one Millie could really count on. Thank God for Gregory.

Her thoughts returned to the present. "Do you have anything else going on this weekend?"

Gregory shook his head. "Just working on my house. I've painted the living room and the dining room is next."

Millie noticed that Gregory's voice had taken on a sad note. "Are you thinking about Marlys, and that if it had worked out with her, she would be helping you with the house?"

"No, not at all. I'm over her. If she ever does come to mind, it just reminds me how stupid I was."

Millie reached over to lay a hand on his arm. "I'm sorry it turned out the way it did."

"It was for the best, Gran. She lied to me. She wasn't who she said she was, at all."

"I know." Millie nodded.

Marlys Stuart had made up a false pedigree to impress Gregory and the rest of the Linscott family. She told them she came from a socially prominent family in the east, and that her father was a land developer. The truth had come out when an old boyfriend came into town and spotted her. When he heard what she claimed to be, he spitefully told the Linscotts that she was from Los Angeles and that her parents owned a small grocery store. Millie checked out his story and found it to be true.

Millie knew that to some people, Marlys's deception would have been considered harmless, but not to a Linscott. It wasn't so much what she was or wasn't. It had to do with her dishonesty. Honesty was at the top of the Linscotts' list of requirements for everyone they dealt with, either personally or in business.

"You'll find someone else," Millie reassured Gregory.

Gregory dismissively waved a hand. "I'm swearing off women for a while. I'm too busy at work and at home to be out looking for someone new."

"I'm going to be busy, too," Millie said. "I've got to finish planning the reception for our muralist."

After breakfast, Gregory left for his job at the bank. He walked down the maple tree–lined driveway to where he'd parked his white, four-wheel-drive Jeep Cherokee. It was brand new, driven off Tom Canlow's downtown lot only a few weeks ago.

Although money had never been a problem, Gregory usually didn't indulge himself in new cars. In fact, he had one perfectly good pickup truck and one perfectly good economy car sitting at home.

However, a couple of months after the fiasco with Marlys Stuart, when his spirits had been particularly low, he'd driven by Canlow's and spotted the Jeep. He suddenly just had to have it. He took it for a test drive and, upon returning to the lot, quickly negotiated and closed the deal.

14

Owning it did in fact make him feel better. Like now. Just looking at that beautiful piece of machinery put a new spring to his step.

Gregory ran his hand over the Jeep's sparkling white finish and gleaming chrome. Even though he'd owned it only a few weeks, it already had had several washes. Instead of using the services of a commercial car wash, he'd done all the work by hand.

There was not a scratch on the car's surface. He'd made sure of that before driving it off the lot, and he was doing his best to see that it stayed that way. At work, he'd moved from his assigned parking spot to a more remote location at the back of the building where no other cars could park close to him.

Gregory climbed in, inhaling with pleasure the pungent smell of new leather upholstery. He started the engine and pushed the button on his CD player. Reba McIntyre's voice filled the air, another lift to his spirits. Ever since he'd seen the country-western singer at a concert in Spokane, he'd been a fan.

He drove along the winding driveway, through groves of trees bursting with new greenery, until he came to the road leading to Cooperville. He rounded a turn and the city lay before him, streets full of buildings stretching north and south; the dense green foliage of City Park; and, on the out-skirts, the mountain of logs belonging to the Cascade Lumber Company, owned by one of his uncles.

However, he saw everything with only half of his mind. The other half lingered on his discussion with Grandmother about the murals. No, he didn't agree with the expenditure for them, but there was nothing he could do about that. Millie had much more influence in the town than he did.

At the town's city limits, he fell into a solid line of traffic headed for Main Street. The traffic through town just got worse and worse, he thought, as he slowed to a crawl. He'd long been a proponent of rerouting out-of-town traffic so that it bypassed Main Street. So far, though, not enough of the townspeople agreed with him. They were afraid their businesses would suffer. In his opinion, the heavy traffic was just as much a hindrance as too little traffic. He wondered how bad the situation would have to get before people came to their senses.

Finally, he was within one block of the bank. Soon he'd be out of this mess and safely inside his office.

The person in front of him, driving a black SUV, braked suddenly for a yellow traffic light. Gregory jerked his foot from the gas pedal and slammed on his brakes, just in time to avoid hitting the other car. He heard a squeal behind him. His gaze darted to the rearview mirror, filled with the image of a red truck. He hoped the driver was quick on the brake.

The driver wasn't. The truck slammed into his Jeep. There was a loud crunching sound as metal hit metal. Gregory jolted forward in his seat.

At first, he sat there stunned, not quite comprehending what had just happened. Then he came to his senses. He yanked open his seatbelt, then the door, and jumped from the Jeep. Blood pumped hard through his veins as he ran around to the back of the vehicle. The red truck was slowly easing away from the Jeep's rear bumper.

He stared at his bumper. It had a big dent in it.

Gregory's jaw dropped in disbelief at the damage. He'd been so careful and protective of his new, prized possession. It was the other driver's entire fault. Who was the dumb bunny, anyway?

Aware that the driver had exited the truck's cab, he whirled around. Red spots of anger dancing in front of his

16

eyes blurred the image of the other person. Gradually, his vision cleared and he saw that it was a young woman.

"Couldn't you have stopped quicker?" he lashed out at her.

She scurried over to him. "I'm so sorry. I was looking for this address and didn't realize the traffic light had changed." She waved a slip of paper clutched in one fist.

"This Jeep is brand new!" he raged on. "I don't even have the permanent license plates yet." He indicated the temporary license affixed to the back window.

"I see that. And I am sorry. I know how it is with something new. How important it is to keep it new and—and nice."

Gregory doubted that. No one could understand how much this stupid accident had upset him.

She went on. "But it's only the bumper that's damaged; the body is still okay."

"Only the bumper," he muttered. That didn't make him feel one bit better.

She turned away to inspect her truck. "And mine doesn't even have a scratch. It's because of the protective rubber thing that my cousin put on for me," she rattled on. "That's one good thing. Isn't it?"

"Yeah, really."

The light changed. The black SUV in front of him moved ahead. A car behind the red truck honked. "We'd better get out of the way," the woman said. "Then we can exchange information."

"You're darned right. You're going to see that this is fixed."

"There are a couple of parking places around the corner," she said, nodding in that direction.

Still seething with anger, Gregory stalked away and

climbed back into his Jeep.

A few minutes later, he and the woman were face-to-face again, standing on the sidewalk next to their parked vehicles. The woman wrote her information on a piece of paper, balanced on what looked like a thick address book. Gregory did the same, grabbing a sheet from the notebook he always carried in his inside jacket pocket.

Gregory finished first. He raised his head and looked at the woman, really seeing her for the first time. Her hair was a pretty auburn color, with copper highlights where the sun hit it. It was pulled into a ponytail at the nape; but, being the kind of curly hair that defies taming, little tendrils had escaped and hung in corkscrews around her face.

Most of her features were hidden as she bent to write, so he studied the rest of her. She wore a baggy blue cotton blouse and khaki shorts. Between the shorts and clunky, Army-surplus-type shoes were incredibly long and shapely legs. Light hairs shone against a glaze of tan. Involuntarily, Gregory sucked in a breath.

The woman finished writing and glanced up. Wide-set hazel eyes with a touch more green than brown gazed at him. A turned-up nose and bow-shaped mouth gave her a sweet look.

Sweet, hah! This woman who had ruined his new Jeep was anything but sweet. And so what if she did have the best-looking legs he'd seen in a long, long time.

"Here." She handed him her slip of paper. "I'm from out of town, but I'll be staying in Cooperville for the summer. I've written down my local phone number at the Mountain View Inn. In fact, that was the address I was looking for when I—" Her voice trailed away as he glared at her. "Well, anyway . . . I'll phone my insurance company back home about this right away. I'm sure they can fix you up in no time."

"I'd appreciate that," he said grudgingly. He had to admit she'd done everything by the rules. He gave her his paper. She stared at it. Her face went suddenly white.

"Gregory . . . Linscott?" she said, as though she couldn't believe what his name was.

He peered at her. "What's the matter? Have you heard of me? I thought you were from out of town?"

"I—no, I haven't, uh, heard of you. And, yes, I am from out of town."

She still looked stricken. Maybe it was a delayed reaction to the accident. Gregory studied the paper she'd given him. It said her name was Julie Foster. Well, he'd never heard of her, either. He stuffed the paper into his notebook and tucked the notebook in his inside jacket pocket.

"I guess that does it, then." He turned on his heel and headed back to his Jeep.

"Any problems, just call me," she said to his back. "I'll be at the Mountain View Inn—if I ever find it."

Her comment hinted that she'd appreciate him giving her directions. But Gregory made no reply. He didn't care if she found her destination or not.

Chapter Two

Julie watched the man whose Jeep she'd just rear-ended walk away from her. Despite the troublesome situation, she couldn't help but notice how attractive he was.

His broad shoulders filled out his gray suit jacket very nicely. His hair was a thick, rich black. Although his back was to her now, in her mind's eye, she could still see his handsome face with its high forehead, long-lashed brown eyes, and firm chin.

She stared at the paper he had handed her.

Gregory Linscott.

Reading his name again brought her down to earth in a hurry. If she had to literally run into someone in Cooperville, and on her first day in town, why did it have to be a Linscott?

He must be related to Millie Linscott, who was head of the Murals Committee, with whom she was to work closely while she was here. The Linscotts were a close-knit family that practically owned the town of Cooperville. So, what was Gregory's relationship to Millie? Julie hoped it was a distant relationship.

She raised her gaze in time to see Gregory's profile as he climbed into his Jeep. His mouth was turned down in a thoroughly disgusted look. He'd probably never forgive her for running into his prized vehicle.

Her mother had said the Linscotts were good at carrying grudges. Well, it hadn't taken her long to put that to the test.

Julie watched Gregory Linscott wheel from his parking place. Returning to her truck, she settled disconsolately into the driver's seat. She put her head in her arms and leaned on the steering wheel. She felt like crying. What a way to start her big adventure.

The accident had definitely been her fault. As she'd told Gregory, instead of watching traffic, she'd been looking at the slip of paper that had the Mountain View Inn's address written on it when she'd run into his Jeep. Not just any old Jeep, but his brand new one. He'd firmly pointed that out.

Julie heaved a deep sigh and straightened up. There was no use sitting here worrying about what was already done. She'd better be on her way. She started the truck's engine and returned to Main Street.

After stopping to ask directions at a service station, she finally located the Mountain View Inn, a two-story, chateau-style building several blocks from the town's business district. Once Julie reached her second-floor room, she took time only to set down her luggage before phoning her Seattle insurance agent. She gave the required information about the accident, adding that her truck had sustained no significant damage.

That done, she phoned Fred Hoskins at the Fairview Art Gallery. A member of the Murals Committee, Fred was her main contact in Cooperville.

"Welcome, welcome!" Fred said. "We're so glad you're here."

"So am I," Julie said, some of her eagerness returning.

"How was your trip over here?"

"It was, ah, fine." Julie didn't want to go into any details about her accident with Gregory Linscott and quickly changed the subject. "I'm looking forward to meeting with the Murals Committee tomorrow."

"That's good to hear, but we've decided to postpone our first meeting till Monday. However, there is a reception in your honor tomorrow evening."

"A reception for me?" Julie was both surprised and impressed.

"Yes, at Millie Linscott's home. It's quite a grand place, one of the oldest estates in the area."

"Oh."

Julie's excitement faded. That wouldn't fit into her plan to stay as far away from the Linscotts as possible. But, of course, she couldn't refuse to attend. That wouldn't make a good impression on the committee at all.

"That's really nice of Mrs. Linscott," she said, pumping enthusiasm back into her voice.

"I'll pick you up around five. It's a buffet supper, so bring your appetite."

"Should I dress up?"

"No, we're pretty casual around here."

"Okay. Thanks, Fred. See you tomorrow at five."

Julie called her mother next and told her she'd arrived safely. "I've already met one of the Linscotts," she admitted.

"So soon? How?"

"We, ah, had a little accident on Main Street." Julie briefly explained the details. "I'm not sure just who Gregory is or how he's related to Millie."

There was silence on the other end of the line, while her mother apparently thought this over. "I don't know, either. I must admit I've tried to forget about them because the memories were so painful. But, oh, Julie, now I'll really worry!"

"Relax, Mom, it'll be all right. My insurance will take care of Gregory's Jeep. With any luck, I'll probably never have to deal with him again."

"I hope you're right, dear."

22

Her phoning chores done, Julie unpacked her clothing and hung it in the closet. The room looked comfortable, although a little cramped, with a queen-size bed, a sofa, two chairs, and a round table. In one corner stood a microwave oven and a small refrigerator.

Looking out the window, Julie saw several distant mountain peaks of purplish rock with zigzagging patches of snow, which accounted for the inn's name. From her earlier research of the area, she knew the peaks to be the tail end of a long range that originated in Canada, some seventy miles to the north.

This certainly was a pleasant change of scene from what she was used to in the city. From her apartment windows there, all she could see were other buildings nearby. Coming to Cooperville had been a good idea, for more reasons than just the murals project.

If only she hadn't had that stupid accident. If only the Jeep's driver hadn't been Gregory Linscott.

Put it out of your mind. Yes, you made a mistake, but don't let it ruin your entire time here.

At the Cooperville Bank, Gregory signed his name to the loan application he'd been working on. He put it aside and plucked another from the In basket on his desk. Reviewing loan applications was his principal task at the bank. This one was for the Sussmans, who wanted to add an eating area to their bakery.

Gregory thoroughly approved. Despite the traffic problem, anything that brought more business into the downtown area was fine with him. The several strip malls on the town's outskirts were okay, but he didn't want the original business district to become a ghost town, as happened with some other small towns he'd visited.

23

Cooperville meant a lot to the Linscotts. Over the years, through economic ups and downs, it had been his family that kept the town going. Either a Linscott or a shirttail relative owned all the larger businesses, from the bank to the lumberyard to the cattle farms.

Gregory had grown up in Cooperville, but had left to attend Seattle's University of Washington. After a taste of big city life, he'd thought he might like to live there permanently. However, his grandmother had expected him to return home and help run the family businesses. Gregory had complied. Now, he was glad he had. This was where he belonged.

Then why did he feel so restless lately? Especially today it had been hard to buckle down to work. His gaze strayed to the window. Through the slats in the blinds he could see the back parking lot. Way over in one corner sat his Jeep. He looked at it and winced. The accident. That darn woman, that Julie somebody, had ruined his day.

Deep down, though, he understood he had overreacted to the accident. There was no way the Jeep could forever escape door dings, scratches, and bumps. It was unrealistic to hope otherwise.

It was just that he hadn't wanted the damages to start so soon. He hadn't even had the car a month yet.

Get a grip and quit whining.

Gregory turned back to the Sussmans' application. He tried to focus on it, but kept seeing instead the young woman from this morning. Pretty auburn hair, hazel eyes on the greenish side, and those long, gorgeous legs. Julie what's-her-name. Gregory pulled the note she'd given him from his shirt pocket. Julie Foster, that was her name, although he didn't know why he cared.

She'd said she was from out of town, but would be staying here for the summer, at the Mountain View Inn. He wondered if he'd see her again around town. Probably. In a small town such as Cooperville, you eventually crossed paths with practically everyone.

Forget Julie Foster! You don't want to see her again.

Gregory rubbed a hand across his forehead in sudden confusion. Did he or didn't he want to see her again? What was going on here?

Frustrated, Gregory put the loan application aside. He stood and picked up his coffee mug. A walk to the employees' lounge and a fresh cup of coffee would get him back on the work track.

"Did you get a chance to look over our fair town today?" Fred Hoskins shifted his gaze from the road to glance at Julie. A few minutes earlier, he had picked her up at the Mountain View Inn to attend the reception in her honor at Millie Linscott's.

Julie nodded. "I drove downtown and walked the main streets. You have a wonderful town. I love all the old buildings and the trees along the sidewalks."

Fred smiled appreciatively. "It'll be even better when we add your murals."

Julie inquired about his art gallery, and he told her about the landscape paintings of a Canadian artist he had taken on. While he talked, Julie studied his profile: high forehead, sparse black hair graying at the temples, a salt-and-pepper mustache, and the beginnings of a double chin. She guessed he was somewhere in his fifties.

As Fred continued to talk, Julie's thoughts wandered ahead to the reception. The gesture was nice of Millie, but Julie wished she hadn't gone to all the trouble. The farther away she stayed from the Linscotts, the better. She was here to work, not to socialize, especially with them.

25

Also, the fact that Fred had called Millie's home an estate was intimidating. She glanced down at her white pullover sweater and navy blue skirt, hoping she looked presentable. Fred had said the dress for the reception was casual, but Julie's casual clothes were her painting clothes; jeans, shorts, and big, loose shirts. Fortunately, she'd thrown in this outfit at the last minute. She must've had a sixth sense that she would need it.

After leaving the town behind and traveling along a tree-shaded, winding road that led up a hill, Fred turned onto a road marked Private. Julie glimpsed a chain-link fence all but hidden by flowering vines and thick bushes. The road wound through a forest of evergreens. Each time they rounded a curve she expected a house or some sign of habitation, but she saw only more trees and the road ahead of them. Millie Linscott certainly liked her privacy, that was for sure.

At last they reached the house. Julie gazed up at a two-story combination of cedar wood and gray limestone, huge windows, and deep, overhanging eaves. The house defied any architectural category that she could think of. Yet, unusual as it was, she could tell it had been planned right down to the placement of the last stone and board.

Fred pulled his car into a line of other vehicles parked in the circular driveway. "A bit of an oddity, isn't it?" he said, gesturing toward the house.

"It's different, all right."

"Originally, this was a large farmhouse that Cyrus built. He was Millie's first husband. One addition after another turned it into a real mishmash. Finally, after Cyrus was gone, an architect relative convinced Millie to let him create a new home altogether. This was the result. Quite pleasing to the eye, I think. And wait till you see the art-work inside. As an artist yourself, I'm sure you'll really appreciate it. Millie's quite a collector."

A maid of around Julie's age, dressed in black slacks and a crisp, white blouse, opened the door. "The party's out back," she told them, stepping aside to allow them to enter.

"Thanks, Letita. I know the way," Fred said.

Letita nodded and left them to continue on by themselves. Fred led Julie across the slate entry to a beige carpeted hallway. He paused at the doorway to a large living room. "Look at that Georgia O'Keeffe." Fred pointed to a picture of pale pink flowers hanging on the far wall.

Julie studied the painting, then let her gaze glide over the rest of the room. A granite fireplace took up most of one wall. Adjacent to that, a winding stairway led to a balcony that surrounded the room on three sides. Overhead, a cut-glass chandelier hung from a high-beamed ceiling. The décor was done in pastel shades that complimented the O'Keeffe painting.

"Very nice," she commented.

They continued on to the kitchen, where caterers were arranging plates of smoked salmon and sandwich appetizers. Double doors led outside to a covered patio full of people. The scent of roses from a nearby bed of flowers filled the air.

Julie didn't even have time to survey the crowd thoroughly before her gaze lighted on a tall, dark-haired man talking to a woman with pale blond hair. Her heart skipped a beat.

It was him.

Gregory Linscott.

Chapter Three

Julie's mouth went dry. Her feet itched to run back into the house, out the front door, and down the long, winding road that had brought her here.

You're not going to run away! You're going to face him calmly. You made a mistake earlier, but you did everything you could to make it right.

As she gradually got over the shock of seeing Gregory Linscott again, Julie realized that he had the same heart-stopping effect he'd had on her when they'd first met yesterday. His thick, dark hair gleamed in the late afternoon sunlight. His broad shoulders were clearly outlined under a lightweight tan shirt, as were his firm hips and thighs under snug-fitting brown slacks.

As Gregory laughed at something his companion said, he turned casually in Julie's direction. The instant his gaze lighted on her, his laughter faded away. His brows knit; his mouth turned down.

Before Julie could decide whether she wanted to return his frown, or to try to melt it with a smile, she heard Fred say, "Oh, there's Millie." She turned to see a tall, long-limbed woman hurrying toward them.

"Our guest of honor is here!" Millie Linscott took Julie's hand and pressed it between both of her own.

"Hello, Mrs. Linscott."

"We're so glad you're here, my dear. And, please, call me

Millie." Julie nodded her agreement.

She guessed Millie Linscott was somewhere in her early to mid-seventies. She looked stylish and sophisticated, yet casual, in mauve slacks and matching silk blouse. She wore her silver hair in thick waves combed back from her face. Her lively brown eyes reminded Julie of Gregory's. But then, she had known the two somehow were related.

"It's really nice of you to have this reception for me," Julie said.

"I thought it would be a good way for people to get to know you." Millie turned to Fred. "Thanks for bringing Julie to the party. You'll excuse us, though, won't you? I want to introduce her around."

"Sure, sure." Fred gave a genial wave of his hand. "I'll get some punch and something to eat."

"I made sure we have those cheese blintzes you like," Millie told him.

"You spoil me, Millie."

"You're on my committee. All my committee members are very special to me." She grasped Julie's elbow. "Come, my dear."

Julie expected to be led to a nearby group that included a couple of the Murals Committee members whom she recognized from when she had come to Cooperville to be interviewed for the position. But Millie marched directly over to Gregory and the blond-haired woman instead.

Oh no! I'm not ready for this!

Of course, there was nothing she could do but follow Millie. Julie's heart thudded as they stopped in front of Gregory and his companion.

"This is my grandniece, Helen." Millie gestured toward the woman. "She's a model."

"Pleased to meet you." Helen pushed a strand of her pale

blond hair behind one ear. She was almost as tall as Gregory and had the brittle thinness befitting her profession. Her outfit of white polo shirt and tan linen shorts and matching jacket looked stylish and expensive.

Millie turned to Gregory. "This is my grandson, Gregory."

Grandson.

Julie's heart sank. She'd been hoping Gregory was only a distant relative of Millie's. And here he was her grandson, of all things. Judging by the way the older woman beamed at him, he was a favorite one, too.

Julie sucked in her breath as she met Gregory's brown-eyed gaze. He wasn't frowning quite as much as before, but he didn't look overly friendly either. Before she could decide whether or not to mention having previously met him, he spoke. "Julie and I are already acquainted."

"Really?" Millie raised her eyebrows and looked from Gregory to Julie.

Gregory waved a hand, as though it were unimportant. "I'll tell you about it later."

Thankful he hadn't brought up the accident, Julie sighed with relief.

Gregory turned to her. "Nice to see you again," he said with icy politeness.

"You too," she replied.

"You'll be seeing a lot of Gregory," Millie said. "He works at the bank."

"Oh?" Julie shot Millie a puzzled look. What was she talking about? Julie wasn't going to have anything to do with the Cooperville Bank while she was here.

"I'll try to keep out of your way when you're painting the mural," Gregory said, with a meaningful look.

Julie spread her hands. "Wait a minute. I don't understand. I'm painting a mural at the bank? I thought the three murals were for the library, the museum, and the theater."

Millie said, "Oh, didn't Fred tell you? We've decided to have the third mural on the bank's wall instead of on the museum's. There will be so much more visibility at the bank, since it's right on Main Street."

"Why, no, he didn't tell me." Julie's stomach lurched as the implication of this news sank in. Contrary to what she had told her mother, she would have to be involved with the Cooperville Bank, after all. Not only that, she would have to endure at least some interaction with Gregory.

Millie said, "Oh, well, that's Fred. He is forgetful, sometimes. I'm sorry you didn't get the word. But, surely, it doesn't make any difference to you, does it? You haven't done any preliminary sketches, have you?"

"No, I was waiting till I got here and could do some research," Julie mumbled.

"I hear you're from Seattle," Helen said. "I've had some assignments with a few of the department stores there. The big city is sure a change from Cooperville."

That led to a discussion of Helen's modeling work. Julie learned that, in addition to modeling for clothing catalogs, she also participated in fashion shows in larger cities, such as Seattle and Spokane.

At last, Millie interrupted, saying she wanted to introduce Julie to the other guests.

As they walked on, Millie whispered to her, "Gregory's not as supportive of the murals project as I had hoped, but he promised to cooperate when you do the one at the bank. And I'm guessing when he sees how beautiful they are and how much they add to the town, he'll change his mind."

Oh, great, he doesn't like the murals idea. Now I have two strikes against me where Gregory Linscott is concerned.

31

The next half-hour was a blur of introductions. Many of the guests belonged to the large Linscott family. They all were cordial and seemed genuinely interested in Julie and the murals she was to paint for the town.

One person who caught her interest was Millie's older sister, Violet Everton. She had the same silver hair as Millie, and the brown eyes that seemed to run in the family, but she lacked Millie's energy and vivacity. Julie wondered if perhaps she might be ill.

"Millie speaks so highly of you," Violet said, giving Julie's proffered hand a limp shake. "Please sit down and let's chat." She gestured to the rattan chair next to hers, sitting on the edge of the patio, apart from the others.

Julie sat, settling back against the cushions. It felt good to be off her feet for a change. "That's nice of Millie."

"I'm so glad the bank will have a mural," Violet went on. "It will please my husband, Harold. He's one of the original partners who started the organization."

"Is that right?" Julie really didn't want to hear more about the bank, but she realized she'd have to, now that it was to be painted.

"Yes. I'd be glad to tell you more about the bank's beginning, if you'd like. It might be helpful to you."

"Please do," Julie said politely.

"Well, my husband, Harold; Millie's husband, Cyrus; and another man named Joseph Gordon were the three who started the bank."

Violet paused to pick up her glass of fruit punch from a glass-topped end table and take a sip. That left an opening for Julie to ask, "Fred mentioned that Cyrus had passed away, but are the other two still active in the business?"

Violet looked at Julie with sad eyes. "Oh, my, no. Joseph still lives in town, but he's long retired. And my Harold is in a nursing home. He's had several really bad strokes, and I just can't take care of him at home anymore." She bit her lip and looked away.

"Oh, I'm sorry." Julie reasoned that Violet's husband's illness and the stress of caring for him were probably the cause of her lackluster appearance.

"Thank you." Violet mustered a faint smile. "During one of his alert times, I told him about the mural. He seemed excited about it."

They were still talking when Millie and Gregory approached. "How about a tour of the house?" Millie said to Julie. "We have some family portraits that might give you some ideas for the murals."

Julie warmed to the idea. "I'd love to see the rest of your home. And the pictures, too," she felt compelled to add.

"I thought you would. Gregory has volunteered to show you around." Millie beamed at her grandson.

I'll bet he did, Julie thought grimly.

However, she noticed that Gregory's smile looked more genuine than earlier. He seemed more relaxed, too, with his hands resting easily in his slacks' pockets. Still, the thought of being alone with him while he guided her around Millie's home turned her stomach into knots again.

But what could she say? She didn't want Millie to know there had been any trouble between her and Gregory. It didn't appear that he had filled his grandmother in on the accident yet, either. So, she politely excused herself to Violet and followed Gregory across the patio toward the house.

As soon as they were out of earshot of the other two women, Julie said, "Look, you really don't have to do this."

He shot her a frown. "And let you wander around by yourself? That wouldn't be very hospitable of us, would it?"

"It's just that I get the impression you'd be happier if you didn't have to have anything to do with me again."

"The accident was pretty upsetting," he conceded, leading her around some guests who were lined up for drinks at a portable bar. "But later I realized that I overreacted. Like I told you, it's a new Jeep and I wanted to keep it in perfect condition as long as I could."

"I'm the same way about new things." Julie lengthened her stride to keep up with him as he headed for the kitchen door. "When I buy new clothes, I leave them hanging in the closet for weeks before I first wear them. I don't want to risk spilling something on them or getting them dirty. They're never the same afterward."

His eyebrows raised in surprise. "No kidding? I thought I was the only one like that."

"No, I'm the same way. Honestly. My friends tease me about it, but I do it, anyway."

"So we agree on one thing, at least." He held up his hands, fingers spread. "Look, let's put the accident behind us, okay? Especially since we'll be seeing more of each other. With the murals project, I mean."

"Deal."

They exchanged smiles. Julie thought she detected not only politeness but also a bit of genuine warmth in his. The knot in her stomach uncoiled slowly. She was glad she'd brought up the subject and cleared the air.

"Gran has lots of contemporary art you'll be interested in," Gregory told her when they were inside the house.

"I saw one by O'Keeffe on the way in."

"Ah, yes, she's one of Gran's favorites."

As they visited the various rooms, Julie spotted two more paintings by Georgia O'Keeffe, a brightly colored abstract by Jackson Pollock, and a lovely landscape by Andrew Wyeth, plus more by other well-known artists. Despite Gregory's disclaimer at being "no art expert," he was full of interesting tidbits about how each work had been acquired. At least, it gave them something neutral to talk about.

However, she found it difficult to focus on either the fascinating home or the conversation. Little things about Gregory distracted her. The way he quirked an eyebrow when waiting for a reply to a question. The way his thick, dark hair tended to curl at the nape. The way he smiled with one corner of his mouth turning up just a bit more than the other did. The word "charming" popped into her mind.

Her preoccupation with Gregory disturbed Julie. She didn't want to be distracted by an attraction to anyone while she was in Cooperville. She was here to work. That it was a Linscott who affected her this way was totally unacceptable.

Julie struggled to push her special awareness of Gregory into the back of her mind. She was just congratulating herself on succeeding when he casually placed his hand under her elbow to guide her into one of the rooms. From anyone else, the gesture would have gone unnoticed, but Gregory's touch sent a shock wave throughout her entire body.

"The photos Gran mentioned are in here," Gregory said.

"Photos?" Julie said blankly, still reeling inside, still all too aware of his nearness.

"Of the family. For your murals."

"Oh, yes." Heat spread up from the back of her neck and around to her cheeks. Heavens, she was blushing. Why didn't she have better control over her emotions?

As though some unseen force orchestrated their movements, they both paused in the doorway and stared at each other. Time stood still as she gazed into Gregory's eyes, deep brown pools she could easily drown in. Her heart beat furiously. Her mouth went suddenly dry. His hand was still on her arm, for heaven's sake. Why didn't he move away? Why didn't she?

"In here . . . photos . . ." Gregory said distractedly. Then he seemed to come to his senses. He straightened up and stepped aside for her to enter the room.

Julie struggled to catch her breath. Whew! She was glad he had finally let go of her and gave her some distance. She had been about to faint from not breathing properly.

The room they entered was the library. Overstuffed chairs upholstered in tweed cloth invited her to curl up with one of the many books displayed on built-in maple shelving. One wall held a stone fireplace flanked by shelves full of bronze sculptures, mostly of birds; majestic eagles, with their wings spread in flight; graceful herons whose long spindly legs looked too fragile to support them; proud seagulls perched on miniature, rope-bound piling. The smell of old leather mingled with the sweeter scent emanating from a huge, cut-glass vase of roses sitting on a coffee table.

Above the shelves hung framed enlargements of landscape and portrait photographs. Gregory led her to one of the latter, showing a dark-haired man dressed in a navy jacket, white shirt, and navy and maroon tie.

"That's Grandfather Cyrus," Gregory said.

Julie gazed at the painting. So, this was the man who accused her Grandpa Ben of stealing money from the Cooperville Bank. She had to set aside that thought and act as though the portrait had no special meaning for her.

"I can see a family likeness between you and him," she said, noting Cyrus's high forehead, chiseled nose, and forceful chin.

"Right. People say I look more like Cyrus than like my father. By the way, Cyrus is one of the men who started the Cooperville Bank."

"Your Aunt Violet told me about that. She said there were two other partners."

"Yes, Violet's husband, Harold Everton, and Joseph Gordon. Joe is one of the few people involved in our business who isn't related to the Linscotts. Joe and Cyrus became friends when they both attended the University of Washington. After that, Joe moved to Cooperville and the three men got together."

"I should be taking notes," she said, deciding that she could handle this topic of conversation, after all. And, the more she knew about the origin of the bank, the better she could design a mural for it. She opened her shoulder bag and pulled out a small black notebook and a pencil. "Okay, I know that Cyrus died awhile back; that Joe is retired, but is still in town; and that Harold is in a local nursing home."

"Right. Harold's illness has been really hard on Aunt Violet. I call her 'aunt,' even though she's my great-aunt. Gran and I worry about her."

"I noticed she appeared rather stressed. You're right to be worried. But, tell me more about your grandfather."

Gregory leaned against the back of a brocaded chair and crossed his arms over his chest. His handsome faced clouded. "Cyrus's life ended in a tragedy the family never got over."

Sensing his distress, Julie said sincerely, "I'm sorry. Maybe you don't feel like talking about it, then?"

Gregory waved a hand. "No, no; it's okay." He straightened and strode to the fireplace. Staring at the empty grate, he began, "About a year or so after the bank opened, and everything had been going fine, some money turned up missing."

Julie's stomach did a flip-flop. This might not be such a good subject, after all. However, she'd prompted the discussion and she couldn't stop Gregory now without arousing his suspicion. She swallowed hard. "Go on."

"Somehow, Grandfather discovered that their accountant was responsible," Gregory continued. "Instead of turning the matter over to the sheriff, as he should have, Grandfather decided to confront the man himself."

Julie stopped writing, gripping her pencil and holding it poised over the notebook. It must have been her grandfather whom Cyrus had decided to confront. "That was, uh, rather bold of him, wasn't it?"

"Yes, and dangerous. But he didn't want a scandal, because it might be bad for business. He thought he could convince the man to pay the money back. Grandfather was always willing to go the extra mile to help somebody.

"Anyway, he set up a meeting with the accountant, late at night, after the bank had closed. Again, not the smartest thing to do, but that was the choice Cyrus made. The next morning, he was found dead in his office. He'd been hit on the head."

"You mean he'd been m-murdered?" she asked, hardly able to believe what she'd just heard him say.

"That's right, murdered in cold blood."

Cyrus Linscott had been found dead in his office. Murdered.

Gregory's words sent waves of shock rippling through Julie. She had never heard this part of the story. She knew only about the alleged theft. Her mother had never told her Cyrus had been murdered. The room began to close in on her, making it difficult to breathe.

"How awful!" she said, amazed that she was able to keep her outward composure. "Did they, uh, know who did it?"

"The accountant, of course. His fingerprints were all over the murder weapon. It was a bronze horse Gran had given Cyrus to display at the bank. Cyrus was partial to bronze. We still have most of his collection." He gestured to the shelves of birds that Julie had noted earlier.

But the bronze statues were of the least interest to her now. "What happened to the accountant?" she asked and held her breath as she waited for his answer.

Gregory turned to look at her, his brown eyes burning with amber lights of anger. "Just what should have happened. He was arrested and charged with murder."

"And did he stand trial?"

"That's the bad part. A crafty lawyer actually got the judge to agree on bail. It was posted, probably with the embezzled money." He gave a short, humorless laugh.

"But what about the trial?" Julie persisted.

"There was no trial. Once he got out of jail, the guy skipped town immediately. The authorities tried, but they never tracked him down. After the law quit looking, the family hired private detectives, but none of them could find him, either. So, he's still out there somewhere, if he's still alive. That was, after all, forty-odd years ago. Anyway, justice was never done in Grandfather's death."

"It's a shame the murderer got away with it," Julie murmured.

"You're darn right it is! If that guy is still living and should be stupid enough to show his face here again; or, for that matter, if anyone connected with him comes around—" Gregory stopped, but his balled fists aptly finished his thought.

Julie suddenly realized that Gregory had never referred to the accountant by name. Perhaps there was still a chance her grandfather was not the man in question. Summoning her courage, she said, "You keep calling him 'that guy.' What was the man's name?"

"His name was Benjamin Gabriel."

Chapter Four

Having her worst fear confirmed was suddenly too much for Julie. "Oh, no!" she exclaimed. Her pencil slipped from her fingers and bounced onto the Oriental carpet. She clutched at her notebook to keep it from dropping, too.

"What's the matter?" Gregory scrambled to retrieve her pencil. He handed it to her, and their fingers brushed. But her emotions were in such turmoil that the effect of another physical contact with him was lost on her.

"Ah, what happened to your grandfather is so—so sad," she managed to say. She bent her head and, although her hand shook, scribbled in her notebook. She hoped Gregory wouldn't notice the hot flush creeping over her face.

Get yourself together. You must not let Gregory know you have a personal stake in what he just told you!

But, oh, the news had hit her with the force of lightning. She had no idea her grandfather had been a suspected murderer. She knew he'd runaway from Cooperville because he'd been accused of embezzlement, but not of murder!

Julie couldn't wait to talk to her mother. She would call her the minute she returned to the inn. Eleanor had a lot of explaining to do.

"Yes, it is sad," Gregory said. "Cyrus never saw the success of his venture with the bank, which went on to flourish despite the missing money. He never saw his son, my father, grow up, or even met me, his grandson. He never got to grow old with his wife, either, while Ben Gabriel got off scot-free."

The raw bitterness in Gregory's voice made Julie cringe. "I can understand how this must have affected your whole family." She struggled to focus only on the Linscotts' experience. She would deal with her own side of the story later. Right now, she must pull herself together enough to get through the rest of the evening.

Gregory shrugged. "Well, what's the use of going on about it? It won't change anything."

"Why don't we talk about something else?" Julie was just as eager to change the subject as he was. "Do you have any photos of the bank as it looked back then? Or of the other buildings I'm to paint, the library and the theater? Photos will help me to get ideas for the murals."

Tension lines around Gregory's mouth softened as his lips curved into a smile. "We do. There are some stored in the credenza." He crossed to a handsome oaken storage chest and pulled a door open by its ornate ring handle. The shelves inside were stacked with photo albums.

Gregory pulled out several and set them on top of the credenza. "Take a couple of minutes to look through them, see if there's anything you think you might be able to use."

"Thanks." Julie took the albums to a chair, sat down, and flipped through the pages. The subjects of the photos barely registered on her, though, as the startling and disturbing story Gregory had just told her played over and over in her mind.

She somehow survived the rest of the tour and the buffet dinner. She made polite small talk with the guests. But inside, she was dying to return to the Mountain View Inn and call her mother.

"So what do you think of our Julie?" Millie asked Gregory

41

when the party was over and the guests had left.

He folded a metal chair and stacked it with some others against the patio wall. From the kitchen drifted the clatter of dishes, silverware, and pots and pans, as the caterers cleaned up and prepared to depart. He carefully measured his words before replying to Millie.

"I thought she was very nice."

Nice was a safe word when you didn't want to commit yourself one way or another. He didn't want to say that once he had gotten over the shock of finding out she was the same woman who'd run into his Jeep, he had found her very attractive.

He'd tried hard not to notice. But it was impossible to ignore that abundance of curly auburn hair, pretty hazel eyes, and soft, bow-shaped mouth. Also, the short skirt she'd worn had given him another opportunity to admire her long, shapely legs.

"What's this about you two having met before?" Millie asked, jolting him from his reverie.

Again, Gregory measured his words. He knew the murals project was dear to his grandmother's heart; and although he didn't agree with it, he had promised to cooperate. He didn't want to upset her by making her think he had another objection to Julie Foster.

"We had a slight accident in town yesterday," he said cautiously, and explained briefly what had happened.

Millie's forehead wrinkled in distress. "Oh, dear. I know how much that Jeep means to you."

He nodded. "But I must admit she handled it well. We exchanged information and she called her insurance company right away, as she promised. They called me this morning. I'll get some estimates and get the bumper fixed. It will all work out."

"I'm glad you're getting it settled and taking it so well. Accidents will happen, as we all know. So, how did the tour of the house go?"

"Okay." Gregory stood aside as one of the women caterers came out to remove a warming tray from the buffet table. "She was naturally interested in your art collection. She has a good background in art, too."

"Don't forget the lid," Millie said to the caterer. As the woman nodded and grabbed up the silver cover, Millie turned back to Gregory. "How about the photos in the library?"

"We looked at those on the wall and she paged through a few of the albums from the credenza." He paused to gaze thoughtfully at the flower garden, where tall rose bushes nodded their blossoms in the light breeze. Beyond the yard, hazy blue twilight was fast fading to a darker shade as night approached. "She seemed much moved by what happened to Grandfather Cyrus. In fact, she got all red and choked up. It was kind of strange."

"It's a very sad story," Millie replied, her eyes clouding. "As an artist, Julie is a sensitive person and I'm not surprised that she was emotionally affected. I take that as a good sign."

A good sign regarding what? Gregory wanted to ask. But he really didn't want to discuss Julie Foster any longer. He was already confused enough where she was concerned.

On the one hand, he wished she and her troublesome murals project would somehow just go away. On the other, he had to admit that tonight he'd been drawn to her. He remembered those moments of camaraderie they'd shared. Imagine, both of them being fanatics about their new possessions. That had been a pleasant surprise.

When he'd taken her by the elbow, a casual, polite gesture he would have used with any woman he was showing around, he'd been jolted by an awareness of the contact. It was almost as if it had been something intimate, although he couldn't see how that was possible. His fingers gripping her elbow? Please!

Then there were those long moments in which for some reason they'd both stopped in the doorway to the library and gazed into each other's eyes. Gregory could still feel the heat that had radiated between them.

He shook his head to clear away the images. He'd better get busy and stop daydreaming. He picked up another chair and added it to the stack against the wall.

"You lied to me," Julie told her mother over the phone later that evening. She sat on her bed at the Mountain View Inn, pillows propped up behind her back. Outside the window, the mountain peaks were silhouetted against a sky in which stars had popped out one by one. However, at the moment, Julie had little interest in nature or the fabulous view. All her attention was wrapped up in the phone call.

"No," Eleanor insisted. "I just didn't tell you everything there was to tell about Grandpa Ben."

Julie twisted the phone cord around her finger. "Yeah, you left out one small detail—he's a murderer." Sarcasm laced her voice. "You told me he ran away because he was accused of stealing money, not because he had killed someone."

"Grandpa always maintained his innocence about both charges, and I believed him," Eleanor said.

"Gregory said his fingerprints were found on the murder weapon. It was a bronze horse."

"Yes, I know about that. But Grandpa said his prints were there because earlier he'd carried the statue into Cyrus's office. Cyrus asked him to move it from where it had been displayed to somewhere else. I guess it was a special gift from Millie, and Cyrus wanted it near him."

"But Grandpa ran away," Julie said. "He was a coward."

Eleanor remained silent, neither confirming nor denying the charge. Then her heavy sigh reverberated in Julie's ear. "I'm really sorry you had to find out this way."

"Why didn't you ever tell me?"

"Because I didn't want you to think of your grandfather as a murderer. It was bad enough that you never had the opportunity to know him. But I wanted to give you some explanation of why he wasn't in our lives, one that was as close to the truth as possible. So I told you only that he was suspected of stealing money. Would knowing the entire story beforehand have made you change your mind about taking the job?"

"I honestly don't know," Julie said. "But it's too late for that now. I'm here and I have to make the best of it."

"I'm really sorry, Julie," her mother said solemnly. After a pause, she added, "Are you going to tell the Linscotts who you are and your relationship to Grandpa Ben?"

"I don't know that, either. I'll have to think about it."

Julie hung up and put her head in her hands. What a mess this was turning out to be. Her grandfather, not just a thief, but a murderer as well.

She had seen Ben Gabriel only once in his lifetime. When she was ten years old, she and her mother had taken the train across the country to visit him in New York City, where he worked as a rooming house janitor. She remembered him as a tired, worn-looking man with gray hair, leathery skin, and stooped shoulders. Yet, when they were introduced, his bright smile lighted up his face. He'd proudly given her a present, a stuffed dog with a red bow. She'd treasured it and still had it at home.

Before that trip, her mother had told her only that her grandmother was dead, and that her grandfather lived far away. Several years later, when Eleanor apparently thought

Julie was old enough to know more, she confided that a long time ago, Ben had been accused of stealing some money. He swore he was innocent. However, certain he would be convicted of the crime, he had taken his daughter Eleanor and run away. He'd stopped in Seattle long enough to visit Eleanor's Aunt Bea, who was his wife's sister. Leaving the child with her aunt, he had vanished and was never heard from again.

Julie remembered that Aunt Bea always frowned when Grandpa Ben's name came up in conversation. Nor would she answer Julie's questions about him. "Ask your mother," was always her reply.

Eleanor told Julie how surprised she was, after so many years had passed and she was grown and with a child of her own, to hear from her father. He had apparently traced her whereabouts, or perhaps he always had been surreptitiously keeping track of her. Whatever, he had contacted her, using his assumed name of James Rhodes, and arranged the meeting in New York.

After that, there had been only occasional written communications. Finally, a few years ago, word had come from an associate of Ben's that he had passed away.

Julie hadn't thought much about her grandfather after his death. When the job in Cooperville came up, her mother told her that was where her grandfather had lived when he had supposedly committed the theft.

Now, she was shocked and upset to find out there was so much more to the story. How would she ever be able to look Millie or Gregory in the eye with this new knowledge? Theft was bad enough, but murder was the worst crime a person could commit.

Julie raised her head and stared at the view through the window. The sky was now full of twinkling stars and a pale moon rose from behind the mountains. Unfortunately, the beautiful scene did nothing to calm her and she turned away to ponder her problem some more.

What should she do?

She could feign a sudden illness, turn the murals project over to her assistant, Audra, and return to Seattle. She could then apply for other, similar jobs in other places.

She really didn't want to do that. Ben Gabriel had been a coward and run away, but that wasn't Julie's nature. She had contracted to paint the murals and had looked forward to being here. So, paint them she would.

However, neither did that mean she would walk up to Millie and tell her she was Ben's granddaughter. She would keep that secret to herself.

It wasn't wrong not to tell, was it? Was keeping quiet the same as telling a lie? Would she be committing what the Bible called a "sin of omission"? Julie had always been confused about just what that meant.

Keeping the secret would not hurt anyone, would it? Therefore, it could not be wrong. That was what she decided in the end, anyway.

What had happened was all in the past. Both men were dead. It didn't matter now whether her grandfather was the culprit or not. With any luck, she'd never have to hear Ben Gabriel's name spoken again while she was in Cooperville.

"I won't have Ben Gabriel included in the bank's mural!" Millie Linscott banged her fist on the table for emphasis. Her fierce, brown-eyed gaze swept over Julie and the three other members of the Murals Committee, of which Millie was the chairperson.

Sitting at the opposite end of the table, Julie ducked her head and busied herself with the notes and sketches she'd been making. No way did she want to meet Millie's eyes. No telling what might show on her face.

It was the Monday following the reception, and Julie was meeting with the Murals Committee in the Cooperville Museum Archives Room. They were surrounded by book shelves and large file cabinets. The room had that musty smell Julie always associated with museums. "We must be historically accurate." Nora Martindale responded to Millie's outburst. "If we include the original bank employees, it has to be all of them."

Julie had earlier noted that Nora, the town's librarian, was a stickler for accuracy. She also didn't hesitate to voice her opinion.

Nora's appearance also commanded attention. In her fifties, she dyed her hair a rich mahogany color and wore bright colors, like today's royal blue sweater and slacks.

"What do you think, Fred?" Millie asked the only male member of the committee.

Fred Hoskins's mustache twitched as his gaze darted away from Millie's probing eyes. "I don't know," he finally said. "I wasn't here when all that trouble happened."

"I know that," Millie snapped. "But you could have an opinion."

"Sorry, but I don't," Fred said.

Millie turned to the museum's curator. "Abby?"

Abby Hawthorn was busy looking through files of old photos for pictures for Julie. Although in her seventies and past retirement age, Abby was still the museum's director. While Nora Martindale stood out in a crowd, Abby easily faded into the background. A petite woman barely five feet tall, she favored pleated skirts and cardigan sweaters in pastel shades. Today's outfit was a pink and gray combination that blended in with her gray hair. Pink-framed reading glasses

48

hung by a silver chain around her neck, and the faint aroma of lavender perfume surrounded her.

Abby looked up and faced Millie with troubled eyes. "Well, I do think accuracy is important, but I also understand how you feel about what happened. That was a terrible time for you."

"So?" Millie probed.

Abby wrung her hands. "Oh, I just can't make up my mind. I'm sorry!"

Millie sat back in her chair and rolled her eyes at the ceiling. "I can see I'm not going to get much help from any of you. Julie, what do you think?"

"Me?" Julie squeaked, startled to be included in the debate. She cleared her throat and focused on restoring her voice to normal. "It's not for me to decide. They're your murals. You tell me what you want and I'll design and paint it."

"But Gregory told you what happened to Cyrus. Surely, you can understand my point of view?" Millie's voice clearly beseeched Julie to come over to her side.

Julie shifted uncomfortably on the hard wooden chair. "I do understand. But, really, it's better if I stay neutral. Please leave me out of it."

Millie sighed and looked at her silver-banded wristwatch. "It's nearly lunchtime. Let's table it for now. Julie, go ahead and design the other two murals. Fred, you see about getting the library wall prepped, because that will be the first one to be painted. Nora and Abby, you're both to help Julie with her research."

"I've already found some photos she might find useful." Abby held up a couple of dog-eared black-and-white photos.

"And I've got a couple of books on Northwest history in mind," Nora put in.

After the meeting and the others had left, Julie lingered while Abby copied the old photographs for her on the museum's copy machine. "This will get you started," the woman said. "But you can come in and use our resources any time you want."

"I really appreciate all your help," Julie said.

"I hope we all can come to an agreement about the bank's mural," Abby went on. "But Millie sounds so firm in her opinion, and she is the committee's chairperson."

"The Linscott family has never really gotten over what happened to Cyrus, have they?" Julie watched the machine hum out a picture of the library when it was first built.

Abby picked up the newly printed copy and peered at it through her reading glasses. "I guess this copy is clear enough. Sometimes this machine doesn't work as well as it could. But, you're right; Cyrus's murder was a big blow to the Linscotts. It was a tragedy for *all* concerned."

Abby's emphasis on the word "all" indicated she knew the other parties involved. Maybe she had known Julie's grandfather, too. They would have been about the same age. Julie wished she dared ask Abby more about the matter. She was curious to know what people other than the Linscotts thought about the tragedy.

However, to probe would be to risk being discovered. No way did Julie want that.

When the copying was finished, Abby put the photos in a large manila envelope and handed it to Julie. "I'm glad you've come to Cooperville," she said, patting Julie's shoulder as she accompanied her to the front door. "I hope we can get to know each other better."

"Thank you," Julie said. "I hope so, too."

"Come back any time. I'm here to help you."

Once outside, the manila envelope tucked securely into

her tote bag, Julie thought about where she would have lunch. Although she had no knowledge of the town's restaurants, she was sure she could find a suitable place to eat along Main Street, only a few blocks away.

Before heading there, however, she decided to take a look at the three walls she was to paint. The buildings all were within walking distance. She headed first to the library, a one-story yellow cement building set back from the street amid towering fir trees. She turned the corner and gazed at the wall to be painted, mentally sketching some ideas she already had. She did the same thing with the theater's mural wall, several blocks away. In contrast to the library, the theater's cement exterior was gray, and three stories in height. Julie's mural would, however, span only to the top of the first floor.

The third building was the bank.

Did she really want to go by there? What if she should encounter Gregory?

So what? As he had said the night of the reception, in a small town such as Cooperville, they were bound to run into each other from time to time. She could handle it. Head high and shoulders thrown back, Julie marched toward the red-brick building.

As she approached, she saw two men coming out the front door. One was a sturdily built older man with white hair, but she hardly noticed him. Her gaze quickly riveted to the other man, who was tall and dark-haired.

It was him.

Gregory Linscott.

Despite her pep talk of a few moments ago, Julie's heart thudded and her mouth went dry. She half-turned, ready to run away. No way did she want to speak to Gregory today. Or any day, for that matter.

Get a grip! She had a perfectly legitimate reason to be there. She needn't be afraid of Gregory Linscott. She doubted he'd buried all his objections about her, but they'd gotten along fairly well at the reception. He'd promised his grandmother he'd cooperate with her while she painted the bank's mural. He'd even told her they should put the traffic accident behind them.

It dawned on her that there was another reason she didn't want to come face to face with Gregory, though, and that was because of the effect he had on her. Even from this distance, the sight of him made her knees go weak.

The midday sun dotted his dark hair with silver lights, while casting flattering shadows over his angular face. One eyebrow quirked in that familiar way of his, and just then he flashed his special smile, one side of his mouth tipping up a little farther than the other.

He looked every bit the professional in tan slacks, a crisp, short-sleeved white shirt—he'd obviously shed his suit jacket due to the warm summer day—and a chocolate brown tie. Even though Julie couldn't tell from this distance, she had the feeling that the color of the tie just matched that of his eyes.

The two men stood in front of the bank's door, deep in conversation. Julie stood transfixed, as though in a dream, as she watched Gregory. People passed her on the sidewalk, cars came and went on the street, but she hardly noticed them. Her tunnel vision saw only one man.

It wasn't until the two men strode along the sidewalk that Julie came to her senses. They were heading straight toward her. Her inner qualms returned. Okay, she wasn't going to run away, but if she could duck out of sight somewhere, she would avoid having to speak to Gregory. She looked frantically around. Ah, there was a bookstore. Its door stood open, welcoming her to enter. Perfect. She turned on her heel and headed toward it.

However, before she could disappear inside the store, Gregory spotted her. "Julie!" he called.

Julie stopped in her tracks and slowly turned around. She raised her eyebrows, hoping to show surprise. "Gregory!"

Gregory motioned to her. "Come over here. There's someone I want you to meet."

There was no way Julie could refuse without appearing rude, and she didn't want to do that. Therefore, she braced herself for another encounter with Gregory Linscott.

Chapter Five

"This is Joseph Gordon," Gregory said when Julie had joined the two men. "I thought you two should meet each other."

Yes, that tie is exactly the color of his eyes. Julie dragged her attention away from Gregory and focused on the other man. "Oh, yes, Mr. Gordon; you're one of the original bank partners, aren't you?"

Joseph Gordon nodded. "I am. But, please call me Joe." In his seventies, Joe had thinning gray hair and a long face with a high forehead. His blue eyes were so pale they hardly had any color at all. He looked casual yet stylish in his outfit of western-style shirt, bolo tie, jeans, and cowboy boots.

Although Joe was smiling at her, Julie sensed an air of aloofness about him. She hoped that didn't mean he shared Gregory's disapproval of the murals project.

"Gregory's been telling me about your murals," Joe said. "I'll be interested to see what you come up with for the bank."

"You met with the Murals Committee this morning, didn't you?" Gregory asked. "Have they decided what's to be in the one for our building?"

"I did meet with them." Julie stepped aside to let a group of people pass by. "They decided on the library's and theater's murals, but some details need to be worked out yet regarding the one for the bank."

Before they could ask her any more about that, she turned

to Joe. "Are you still involved with the business?"

He shook his head. "Not anymore. After Cyrus's death, Harold Everton and I ran it. Eventually, Cyrus's son, Winston, joined us. For a short while, anyway. Until he got the crazy notion he'd rather live on an island in the South Seas. Winston passed away several years ago, as did Cyrus before him. I take it you've heard that story?"

Julie nodded, suppressing a sigh. Yes, unfortunately, she had heard.

"Do you still live in Cooperville?" she asked.

Joe stuck his hands in his jeans' pockets and leaned back on the heels of his boots. "Yes, this is my home. I put my money and efforts into other interests and did pretty well, if you'll pardon a little bragging." He lifted his chin in a gesture of pride. "I hear you're from Seattle."

"Right."

Joe's raised eyebrows indicated he expected her to say more about that, so Julie volunteered a few facts about her background as an artist. She carefully avoided saying anything about her personal life.

Joe continued to watch her intently. After awhile, Julie felt uncomfortable under his gaze. Was there something wrong with the way she looked?

"Is something wrong?" she asked.

Joe shook his head as though to clear his thoughts. "I'm sorry. I know I was staring, but I can't shake the feeling that I've seen you before. Have you been to Cooperville in the past?"

"I was here a couple of months ago for an interview with the Murals Committee, but that's the only other time. I'm pretty sure I didn't meet you then."

"No, I'm sure I'd remember if we had met." Joe thoughtfully rubbed his high forehead. "Maybe it's just that you

55

remind me of someone. I don't know who it is, though. Darn, that's frustrating!"

An alarm sounded inside Julie. Did she remind Joe of her grandfather, Ben Gabriel? Recalling the image of the Ben she'd met when she was ten years old, a man with a wrinkled, leathery face and gray hair, she could see no resemblance to either her mother or to herself. But perhaps as a younger man he had looked quite different.

However, if she did resemble her grandfather, why hadn't someone else seen it? Millie Linscott, for example. Or Millie's sister, Violet Everton.

Julie said brightly, "Well, they say everyone has a twin. Perhaps you've met mine."

"No, it's something else," Joe said. "But, I don't have time to worry about it any more now. I've got to be going."

"It was pleasant meeting you," Julie said.

Joe nodded. "No doubt we'll be seeing more of each other." He turned to Gregory. "Good getting together today, Greg. I'll talk to you soon."

As Joe walked away, Gregory said to Julie, "Yeah, he's a great guy. He's been like a father to me since Dad passed away. He trained me for my job and drops in frequently to see how I'm doing, like today's visit."

"He does seem nice," she agreed, more to be polite than because she really felt that way. Meeting Joe Gordon had left her apprehensive and anxious. That she reminded him of someone would hang over her head like a black cloud. She hoped she wouldn't have to have anything more to do with him.

Gregory cocked his head, as though an idea had just struck him. "I was heading out for lunch. Why don't you join me? After that, if you have time, I'll give you a tour of the bank. Might be useful research for you."

His unexpected invitation startled her. It must have shown on her face, for he said, "Don't look so stricken. It's only lunch."

Julie laughed nervously. "I know. It's just that, considering the accident and how you feel about my project, I didn't think you wanted anything to do with me."

Gregory frowned at the reminder. "I promised Gran I'd cooperate, and that's what I'm trying to do. But if you'd rather not join me, just say so. And you could see the bank some other time and with another tour guide."

"Oh, but I would like to join you now," Julie said quickly. "Lunch would be very nice."

She didn't want to rebuff him and have it get back to Millie. But at the same time she mouthed the words of acceptance, a little chill of fear slithered down her spine. Spending time with Gregory Linscott meant entering dangerous territory. She'd have to be very careful not to slip and say something that would give away her real identity. She'd also have to be careful not to show her attraction to him. It was like walking a tightrope with no net underneath.

Gregory gazed at the young woman sitting across from him, wondering what had possessed him to invite her to lunch. The words had been out of his mouth before he'd realized what he was saying.

Not that he wasn't having a good time. He was. They'd been talking steadily since they'd given the waitress their orders.

And he was comfortable here. Cindy's Cafe was one of his favorite places, an informal restaurant with a 1950s theme, located a couple blocks off Main Street. The hostess, a matronly woman named Martha, had led them to a booth in the back, under huge photos of James Dean, Natalie Wood, and

Sal Mineo from the movie *Rebel Without a Cause.*

They had studied the menus in silence for a few moments. Then Gregory ordered his usual hamburger, while Julie opted for a chicken croissant sandwich.

While they waited for their meals, Julie asked Gregory questions about Cooperville. What the population was, when had it been founded, and so forth, facts he assumed she wanted to know as background for her artwork. Either that or she just wanted to make safe small talk.

Whatever her motive, he enjoyed her company.

He also enjoyed looking at her. She wore an outfit similar to the one she'd been wearing when he'd first met her. Khaki shorts, an oversize, emerald green shirt that picked up the dominant color of her eyes, and those Army surplus shoes. Funny, but he thought her legs looked sexier wearing those shoes than they had in the white sandals she'd worn to the reception.

Her auburn hair was in a ponytail. At least, some of it was. The rest had escaped and curled around her face. On someone else, the hairdo would look messy; on her, it looked great.

"So, there's just the one newspaper in town?"

"What?" He had better pay attention to the conversation.

"Newspaper. Is *The Cooperville Gazette* the only one?"

"Right. It's a weekly."

Julie sipped from her glass of water. "I was thinking they might have archives I could look through. There might be some interesting photos."

"I'm sure they do. The office is on Main Street, not far from here."

Their orders arrived, and silence reigned for a few minutes while they concentrated on eating. Then Gregory said, "So, tell me about you."

Her raised eyebrows told him his question was not welcome. Why? he wondered.

"Like what?" She poked a piece of lettuce back into her sandwich and took a bite.

He shrugged. "The usual stuff. Your family, for starters. Mother? Father? Sisters and brothers?"

"My mother and stepfather live in Seattle. My stepbrother, Tim, is in the Army, stationed in Texas. He's two years older than me. My birth father lives in San Diego. He and my mother divorced when I was six."

"How about grandparents?"

Julie stared down at her plate. "My birth father's parents live in San Diego, too. All the others have passed away." She raised her head and gazed at him with somber eyes. "That's about it. Compared to yours, mine is a really small family."

He grinned. "I guess so. Cyrus was one of eight children; Millie came from a family of five. Most of their siblings and their offspring live in Cooperville, or in one of the neighboring towns. The Linscott clan has really stuck together over the years. Even though we see one another frequently, we have big reunions every two years, usually at Millie's. They're always great fun. It's good to have family ties, I think."

"Yes, it is," Julie agreed. She looked away, as though deep in thought. Another patron put some money in the old-time jukebox across the room, and soon the strains of Elvis Presley's "Blue Suede Shoes" filled the air.

He wondered why she suddenly lapsed into such a serious mood. Perhaps talking about her family had brought up bad memories. Her mother and father's divorce, for example, might be something she'd never gotten over. Divorce was always painful.

He changed the subject. "When did you first become interested in being an artist?"

59

That brought a smile back to Julie's face, which made Gregory feel better, too.

"I think it was back in first grade," she said, "when we were supposed to draw pictures of our family. My drawing had the typical stick figures, you know the kind, but it was such fun. And although I had drawn before, there was something different about that time, taking those big, thick crayons and coloring my pencil drawing. Then, when I brought my masterpiece home, my mother made a big fuss over it and tacked it onto the refrigerator. That made it really special. Believe it or not, I still have that picture, pasted into one of my many scrapbooks. It's all faded from hanging up for so long, but I treasure it to this day."

"That's a good story." Gregory sipped his coke. "I remember those times in grade school, making drawings with crayons. And, yes, they got hung on the refrigerator, too. Must be a ritual everyone goes through."

Julie laughed. "A ritual. That's a good way to put it."

From then on, the conversation stayed on more general topics. Gregory sensed that Julie had relaxed. Although still puzzled about her earlier seriousness, he decided not to worry about it and just enjoy their lunch.

On their way back to the bank, Julie stopped to gaze at some handmade quilts displayed in a gift shop window.

"Some quilts tell stories, the way murals do." She pointed to a quilt with a green background and octagonal pieces of print material sewn onto it in various patterns. "That one shows the different stages in a garden. There are the seeds being sown, then watered with a watering can, and then the flowers growing."

Gregory tilted his head this way and that. "Okay, now I see it." He had always thought of quilts as just colorful bits of fabric sewn together to make, okay, a pleasing pattern, but with no particular purpose in mind. Now, he looked at them with a fresh perspective. "Will the murals you're going to paint here tell stories?" he asked as they strolled on.

"Yes. Each one will contain several vignettes about the building and the town. From the ideas the committee gave me this morning, I'll make some sketches and then have them decide on the final compositions."

"You said there was a problem with the bank's mural," Gregory said. "What's going on?"

Julie's face clouded. "I'm sure the committee will work it out," she said evasively.

They stopped on a corner for a red traffic light. He turned to her. "Come on, tell me what the problem is. Since it concerns the bank, I should know."

Julie heaved a sigh. "Okay, since you insist. They all agree that the scene show the original three partners and their employees. But your grandmother doesn't want it to include that—that man who—who—" She stopped, seeming to choke on her words.

"Ben Gabriel," Gregory supplied, watching the passing traffic without really seeing it. His stomach tensed, as it always did when his grandfather's murderer was mentioned. "And I don't blame her. I agree with her. What about the rest of the committee?"

"Well, Nora opposed your grandmother. She's in favor of historical accuracy."

Gregory nodded. "That sounds like Nora. If you want to know any facts, past or present, she's the one to see. If she doesn't already know them, she can tell you where to find them." The light changed in their favor and together they stepped off the curb.

"Abby and Fred are undecided," Julie said.

"Hmmm, that figures. They're both wonderful people,

61

but it's sometimes hard for them to take a stand. Once, Abby couldn't decide between two candidates for a job in the museum, so she hired both of them. It threw the budget director into a tizzy. And have you seen Fred's gallery? He's got some great stuff, but it's a mishmash of styles."

"I see. Well, anyway, that's why they're at a stalemate."

"I have to say I agree with Gran. I hope she stands her ground."

"I'm sure she will."

"What's your opinion?" he asked.

"I don't think it's my place to have an opinion."

However, her troubled expression told Gregory she did have feelings about it. Of course, she would side with the Linscotts. She was a sensitive, caring person, as Gran had observed the night of the reception.

His gaze lingered on Julie's profile as they continued walking. He liked her upturned nose and the curve of her full lower lip. The sunshine glinted on the corkscrew curls hanging around her ear, turning them to burnished gold.

Something stirred inside Gregory, a feeling he couldn't put a name to, but was there, nonetheless.

They reached the bank. "Are you still up for a tour?" Gregory asked. He hoped she'd say yes. Despite all the loan applications that were waiting for him, he didn't want to leave her just yet.

She looked up at him, a smile forming on her lips. "Yes, if you have time, I'd appreciate looking around."

"I do. I thought seeing the bank's interior would help you with your mural."

Gregory took Julie around the bank, introducing her to the employees as they went along. "The floor plan is basically the same as it was originally," he told her. "We've even kept some of the original fixtures and furniture." He pointed out the high mahogany tables where people made out their deposit slips, and the brass closures to the tellers' cages.

Julie wrote in her notebook. "I'll bring my camera someday soon and take pictures."

He led her into a spacious office. "This is my office. Originally, it was Cyrus's. That old roll-top over in the corner was his desk. In fact, this is the room where he was murdered." He glanced at Julie and saw her face blanch. "You seem to be as upset about what happened as I am," he said.

"I—it was a terrible tragedy." She stopped and bit her lip, then continued in a rush of words. "But I think I've seen enough now. I'd better be going." She stuffed her notebook and pen into her tote bag. Before he knew what was happening, she turned and hurried from the room.

Gregory ran to catch up with her. Although greatly puzzled by her behavior, he decided it was due to her sensitivity. He kept close behind her as she scurried across the bank's main area and through the glass doors.

When they were outside, he took her by the arm, pulling her to a stop. "Julie, wait, please. Is something wrong?"

She kept her eyes downcast. "No, nothing, Gregory. Well, maybe." She finally looked up. "It's just that all of a sudden, being in the room where a murder was committed gave me the creeps. I felt the room closing in on me, and, well, I just had to leave. I'm sorry."

"No, I'm sorry. I shouldn't have mentioned it. I know what you mean. It took me a long time to get over it enough to be able to work there."

"No, no; that's all right. I do want to know the history of the bank. But . . ." Her voice trailed off, and she gave a shrug. "Anyway, thank you for lunch and the tour. You've been very . . ."

"Cooperative?"

She laughed, and the sound of it lifted his spirits. "Yes, just like your grandmother said you'd be."

A sudden impulse seized him, and he said, "How about extending today's tour to some other places around town? I could spare a couple more hours. You asked about the newspaper and archives. I could take you to the office and introduce you to the editor. He's a good friend of mine. And we've got a great city park that I think you'd like."

The thought of his work waiting for him nagged him again, but he brushed it aside. He'd work overtime tonight and make up for taking time off this afternoon. If only she'd say "yes."

She looked startled and spread her hands in protest. "No, thanks. You've done enough. I don't want to trouble you any more."

"It's no trouble. I'd like to do it." Gregory paused, knowing that what he wanted to say next would plunge him into dangerous waters.

What happened to your resolve not to get involved with anyone right away? pestered an inner voice.

He ignored it. "I'm trying to say that I want to see you again."

"Oh, I'll be around." She gave him a wry smile. "You'll see enough of me while I'm painting the murals."

"I don't mean that. I want to see you. You know."

Her smiled faded. "Okay, I get your drift. But our becoming involved on a personal level is not a good idea."

"Why not?"

She looked away and tucked the stray curls back behind her ear. They immediately sprang forward again. Gregory had the urge to reach out and twist them around his finger. He imagined how silky the strands would feel.

"It just isn't," she said.

A sinking feeling hit him in the pit of his stomach. "Did I misread the signals? I thought there was some interest on your part—"

"That doesn't have anything to do with it," she said quickly.

"Then you are. Interested, that is."

"Please, don't push this." Distress wrinkled her forehead.

Something dawned on him, like a light bulb above the head of a cartoon character. "Ah, there's someone waiting for you back in Seattle, is that it? I should have known an attractive woman like you would be spoken for."

"No, there's no one."

"Then what?"

"Well, for starters, I ruined your new Jeep, you hate my murals project—"

He waved a hand to interrupt her. "I can get beyond both of those reasons. I already have. I thought I made that clear. Come on, now, you'll have to do better than that."

"Okay, how about the fact that I'm here only for the summer?"

"Uh-uh. Not good enough. Besides, I'm not asking for a long-term commitment here. I had a good time today and I want to get to know you better."

She looked at him very soberly. "You don't want to get to know me better."

He wrinkled his brow. "I don't understand."

"Just trust me on that. Please, Gregory."

With that, Julie turned and walked away. Gregory stared after her. What was going on? Why wouldn't he want to get to know her better? After spending the past couple of hours with her, there was nothing he could think of that he wanted more.

Then reality hit him. He'd just been rejected. She wasn't interested in him on a personal level, after all. She'd gone to lunch and toured the bank with him because she'd thought she might learn something that would help her with her job.

A feeling came over him that he hadn't experienced since he'd discovered his old girlfriend Marlys' deception.

He felt like a fool. A great big fool.

Chapter Six

As afternoon sunlight streamed through her motel room window, Julie tore a sheet of drawing paper from her large tablet and taped it to her drawing board. She poured the pictures from the manila envelope Abby Hawthorn had given her that morning onto the table. She shuffled through them until she found those that showed the library when it was first established. She lined them up in chronological order, setting aside those she thought would be good for the mural. The one showing the dedication, featuring a group of prominent townspeople, and the one of the first librarian holding a children's story hour particularly caught her eye.

She took out her drawing pencils, erasers, and T-square and set to work making thumbnail sketches inspired by the various photos.

Julie loved to draw. The courses that featured drawing and sketching had been among her favorites in art school. She often became so absorbed in putting pencil or charcoal to paper that she lost track of the time.

Today, however, that wasn't going to happen. The events of the day streamed through her mind like TV reruns. She had hoped to not be reminded that her Grandfather Ben was a suspected murderer; yet at every turn, the subject came up. Seeing the actual room where the murder had occurred was the last straw. Julie had suddenly felt suffocated and had to get out of there.

As if all that weren't bad enough, then Gregory dropped his bombshell that he was personally interested in her. In any other situation, the attention of a man such as Gregory Linscott would have sent Julie into a tailspin of excitement. He was intelligent and interesting, not to say drop-dead gorgeous. She had enjoyed being with him at lunch, and was enjoying the tour of the bank, up until that moment in his office. She would have loved to accept his invitation to extend the outing for a couple more hours, and even get together on another occasion for a planned date.

But, although she ached to, she didn't dare go out with him. Even if he never learned of it, her relationship to the much-hated Ben Gabriel would hang over them like a black cloud.

If she did confess and tell Gregory the truth, she was sure he would want nothing more to do with her. Worse, he would of course pass the information on to Millie. Millie would be outraged. Julie would lose the murals commission, as well as be run out of town on the proverbial rail.

What a dilemma.

Despite her troublesome thoughts, Julie managed to continue working at her drawing board for a couple of hours. Then she decided to take a break and have a cup of tea. She rose, stretched, and filled the little coffeemaker provided by the inn with tap water. She took out the container of tea bags she'd brought with her and chose mint with a hint of tarragon, her favorite. While the water burbled softly in the coffeemaker, she walked to the window and looked out at the peaceful field and the mountains in the distance. Everything would work out, she told herself.

The coffeemaker's red light came on, signaling that the water was ready. Julie returned to it and steeped her tea in one of the inn's white mugs.

As she deposited the spent tea bag into a wastebasket, a movement near the door caught her eye. Turning fully around, her gaze dropped to the tweed-patterned carpet as a slip of paper appeared from under the door.

What was this all about? A little frisson of apprehension skittered down Julie's spine. There was something surreptitious and scary about a note arriving in that manner, as though the bearer didn't want to be discovered.

Don't be silly, she told herself; it was probably just an innocent notice from the management. Maybe a room service order form or a sheet of the discount coupons for nearby restaurants that she'd seen stacked on a table in the lobby.

Julie crossed the room and picked up the paper. It had been cut from a larger piece of lined notebook paper. She unfolded it and stared with horror at the crudely printed message:

I know who you are.

Later that afternoon, Gregory accompanied his great-aunt Violet to the Dayton Nursing Home to visit her husband, Harold. The home sat on tree-shaded acres of property on the outskirts of town. Gregory drove them there in his Jeep. He still hadn't had the bumper fixed yet, but he'd gotten the required estimates and had chosen the shop to do the work. It was just a matter of making an appointment to have it done.

He pulled the Jeep into a slot in the parking lot. They got out and approached the building that Gregory always thought looked like someone's comfortable country home. They climbed the steps to the porch, and entered through the double doors. Violet nodded to the receptionist as they passed by her circular desk.

"I hope Harold's having a better day than yesterday,"

Violet said, as they headed down the hall leading to Harold's room.

"What happened yesterday?" Gregory asked.

"He was so weak he could barely talk. I'm afraid it won't be long now . . ."

Gregory touched her arm. "Please, Aunt Violet, don't think of that today. Let's be in good spirits, for Harold's sake."

"You're right." She turned to him and mustered a smile.

Gregory knew that Violet visited her husband every day. At least once a week, someone from the family accompanied her. Often, he was the one. He didn't mind; in fact, he volunteered. It was hard, though, to see his great-uncle so debilitated from the several strokes he'd suffered.

Harold had always been an active and dynamic man, even after his retirement from the bank. He loved to play golf, to fish, and to build birdhouses and other yard decorations in his home workshop.

It also distressed Gregory to witness the toll the illness was taking on Violet. She, too, was only a shell of her former vivacious and energetic self. Once, she and Gran had looked enough alike to be mistaken for twins. But not anymore. In the past couple of years, Violet had aged twice as fast as Gran had.

Gregory's tension eased as they entered Harold's room and saw him sitting in a wheelchair near the window. At least, he was well enough to be up today.

"Look who I brought with me, darling," Violet said cheerfully.

Harold turned to look at them. "Gregory. S-son, it's . . . always g-good to see you." It was a struggle for Harold to talk, because the strokes had affected the area of his brain that controlled speech.

Harold held out a shaky hand. Gregory winced at the bony feel of Harold's grip. It had always been so firm and confident in days past.

"You're looking good today," Gregory said, and meant it. Despite the rheumy eyes, his great uncle's cheeks sported a bit of color, and his mouth, though paralyzed on one side, had curved into a crooked smile. He was always neatly dressed, too, today in brown slacks, and tan shirt, and a brown and red plaid cardigan sweater.

"Not too b-bad," Harold said.

Harold raised his face to receive his wife's kiss on the cheek, while Gregory pulled up straight chairs for him and Violet. Through the open window came the pleasant sound of water coursing through a courtyard fountain. He glanced outside. A few patients and visitors were grouped around the tulip-shaped structure, chatting and enjoying the sunshine. Beyond that, a couple of nurses pushed patients in wheelchairs along a flower-lined path toward a Victorian-style gazebo.

Gregory turned back to his great-uncle and aunt. They talked about trivialities, things that really didn't matter, but that kept them from dwelling on the awful truth of Harold's illness.

"How is the b-bank?" Harold asked at length. He always asked Gregory about the bank. Even though many years had passed since he'd worked there, he always wanted to know what was going on. Gregory could understand that. Work had been a big part of Harold's life, as it was in his own.

"Good," Gregory said. "We've increased our loans by ten percent this year. The board of directors is doing a study on whether or not we should open a branch in Wilton. That would be something, wouldn't it? Oh, and Joe Gordon stopped by this morning."

Harold nodded. "He came t-to see me. The other d-day. W-what about the mural? Violet t-told me about it."

Gregory nodded. "The young woman who's to paint it came by the bank just as Joe and I were leaving. Her name is Julie Foster, and she's from Seattle. I introduced her to Joe." He paused, recalling the incident, then added, "She reminded Joe of someone, but he couldn't think who."

Violet cocked her head. "Hmmm, I had that feeling, too, when I met her at the reception. There was something so familiar about her, but I couldn't put my finger on it."

Gregory said, "Maybe you saw her when she was here to interview for the job and just don't remember it."

"Possibly," Violet said. "Goodness knows, my memory isn't what it used to be. She's a charming young lady, though. Did the committee decide what will be in the bank's mural, by the way?"

Gregory leaned back and folded his arms across his chest. "No, there's a problem with that. They more or less decided to have a scene showing the original partners and employees, but Gran refuses to have Ben Gabriel included. I must say, I agree with her."

"B-Ben Gabriel," Harold said in a choked voice. His lips moved some more, but no words came out. Splotches of red broke out on his face.

Violet jumped up and poured a glass of water from a pitcher on the bedside table. She held the glass to his mouth. "Here, Harold, drink this." Harold managed to gulp some of the water.

Gregory leaned forward, concerned. "I'm sorry. I didn't mean to upset you, Uncle Harold."

Harold waved a hand and mumbled something unintelligible.

"We'd better change the subject," Violet whispered to

Gregory, as she returned to get more water from the pitcher.

"Right." Gregory turned to Harold and pointed to the TV set mounted to the wall. "There's a baseball game on this afternoon. The Seattle Mariners against San Diego. Going to watch it?"

But Harold was staring out the window. He seemed to focus on the courtyard scene, although it looked to Gregory as though his thoughts were miles away. It took several more tries before he could draw him back to the present and into a conversation.

Later, as he and Violet were on their way out, Gregory said, "I should have known better than to bring up Ben Gabriel's name. None of us has ever gotten over Cyrus's death, and with Harold's condition, it's especially hard on him to be reminded."

Violet nodded. "Last week, when I told him Julie Foster was coming to paint a mural on the bank wall, he seemed excited in a positive way. Maybe I misinterpreted his reaction, though, because it certainly wasn't positive today."

Sitting in a booth at the Mountain View Inn's cafe, Julie picked half-heartedly at her chicken salad. It wasn't that the food was unappetizing. On the contrary, made with fresh chicken and chunks of apples and walnuts, and with a tangy dressing, it was quite tasty. The sourdough roll that came with it was still warm from the oven.

The note that had mysteriously appeared under her door had taken away her desire to eat. Even now, folded up into a small square, it burned a hole in the breast pocket of her shirt. She couldn't get her mind off it.

After recovering from the initial shock of its startling message, she had yanked open the door to her room and peered up and down the hallway. No one was in sight, and the only sound was the clunk, clunk of the ice-making machine in the corner. Still, she had the creepy feeling that someone lurked nearby.

She hurried to the lobby and asked the clerk on duty if anyone had been asking for her. No one had, the woman said. Julie returned to her room, looking over her shoulder all the way down the hall, expecting someone to step out of the shadows and confront her. Back inside her room, with the door securely locked, she tried to get back to her sketching, but couldn't concentrate. She kept staring at the note, as if it were something unreal. Hunger pangs had finally sent her in search of food.

Now that food was in front of her, she could barely eat. Who had sent the note? Who in Cooperville knew who she was? One of the Murals Committee, perhaps. They probably knew more about her than any other townspeople, from the information she had given when she applied for the job. However, as far as she could remember, nothing in that information linked her to Ben Gabriel.

Was the sender Joe Gordon? Maybe he'd finally recalled who she reminded him of, and that someone was Ben Gabriel.

Why had the note been sent? It wasn't threatening. It didn't say, "Get out of town," or, "I'm going to tell everyone who you are." That might have been easier to deal with than not knowing the sender's intent.

What should she do now? Quit her job and run back to Seattle? Julie didn't want to do that. To leave this job uncompleted might ruin her chances of landing future jobs.

She remembered that after she'd learned her grandfather was a suspected murderer, she'd also contemplated running away. Probably, that was a normal first reaction.

Well, she wasn't a quitter then and she wasn't going to be now, either.

The waitress, in her perky green-and-white uniform and with her ponytail swinging jauntily, came by with her coffeepot. "Is everything all right?" she asked, as she refilled Julie's cup. She looked questioningly at the half-eaten salad.

"Just fine, thanks," Julie said, and choked down another bite.

Still in a dilemma, Julie paid for her dinner and returned to her room. As she stepped inside, the phone rang. She froze. What if the caller was the person who had sent the note?

The phone continued to ring. She stared at it, her feet rooted to the floor. Finally, she came to her senses. She must answer it, no matter what. She crossed the room and lifted the receiver. She sucked in a breath. "Hello?"

"Julie?" said Millie Linscott's voice. "I was about to give up."

"I just returned from the restaurant," Julie said. Her heart pounded furiously. Was Millie the sender of the note, calling now to reveal herself and ultimately dismiss Julie from the murals project?

Millie continued, "I've been thinking about you staying there at the Mountain View Inn. It's a nice place, as motels go, and probably the best Cooperville has to offer. But I think you'd be much more comfortable out here."

"At your place?" Julie said, taken completely by surprise.

"Yes, you'd have more space to work, and our entire library at your disposal. We have several guestrooms, any of which I'm sure you'd like. They all have northern exposure. Isn't that supposed to be good for artists?"

"That's right. It's true there isn't a lot of room here for drawing." Julie glanced at the small round table where she'd set up her materials. The large window provided adequate light during the day, but at night, the droplight hanging from

75

the ceiling was a dim substitute.

"I must admit to having an ulterior motive for wanting you to come," Millie said.

Uh-oh, Julie thought with a new sense of alarm. What could that be? "You do?" she queried tentatively.

"Yes. There's a really ugly shed in my yard. It's been there for ages. I considered tearing it down, but never quite got around to it. Now that I've become aware of what murals can do for buildings, I'm glad I didn't. I thought the side that faces the garden could be covered up with a mural. Would you be interested in taking on the project?"

Interested in doing another mural? Of course, she was. If only the job wasn't for Millie Linscott. If only she'd not received that note.

"I don't know." Julie hedged. Which was worse, to stay here where the note sender could easily get at her, or to stay with Millie, where she'd have to be constantly on guard, lest her secret be discovered?

"Please come," Millie said.

Julie knew she had no valid excuse for refusing. None she could reveal anyway.

"I'd love to stay with you," she said.

"I know it'll add some miles to your commute to town, once you get started on the painting. But on the days that you don't have equipment to tote back and forth, you can ride with Gregory."

"Gregory?"

"Yes, he lives on the next property."

Oh, no, now she'd be seeing even more of Gregory.

But it was too late to back out.

"I'll expect you sometime tomorrow afternoon," Millie said. "Do you need any help moving out here? I could let Gregory know."

"No, no, I can manage okay," Julie said hastily. "I'll see you tomorrow."

"Be sure to get here in time for dinner. We eat at seven."

"I'll be there by then."

Julie hung up, wondering if she had done the right thing by accepting Millie's invitation. What if the person who had sent the note continued to badger her at the Linscott home? Would that ultimately lead to Millie's finding out who Julie really was?

How would she get along with Gregory after she had turned him down today? Would he be so angry with her that he would oppose her murals more than ever?

Julie sighed in frustration. It seemed that every move she made in Cooperville plunged her deeper and deeper into trouble.

Chapter Seven

Julie opened her eyes to sunlight filtering through filmy window curtains. For a moment, she couldn't think where she was. Then she remembered she was at Millie Linscott's. She had moved here several days ago. She turned over and plumped the pillow under her head. The bed was cozy and comfortable, and it would be easy to linger awhile, letting her thoughts drift.

However, with much to do, Julie knew she'd better get her day started. She threw back the quilted cover and sat up. Her gaze took in the still unfamiliar room. It was much more spacious and elegantly furnished than her room at the inn.

The bed, dresser, and armoire were modern pieces painted a forest green with brown trim. In one corner, by a window that afforded a view of the mountains, was a sitting area with a floral-printed chaise lounge and two overstuffed chairs. There was even a good-size table with two straight chairs where she could lay out her drawings or sit down to eat or to have a cup of tea. It was all quite luxurious to Julie, who was used to her relatively small and simply furnished Seattle apartment.

The room had its own bathroom, too, where Julie now headed. She loved the old-fashioned, claw-footed tub, where she'd already enjoyed soaking in a couple of hot baths. She stood at the sink and washed her face, drying off with one of several thick, white towels. Underneath her bare feet was a thick-pile carpet to keep her toes warm.

Julie brushed her teeth and returned to the bedroom. She opened the closet, pulled out a clean pair of jeans, and put them on. She thought about the day ahead. She'd been at Millie's for three nights, and already had fallen into the routine of having breakfast with her hostess, then working on her research and sketches in the library. All three days, she had lunched alone, attended to by Hilda the cook, as Millie had gone off to work on her many projects. She had returned in time for dinner, sometimes with a guest or two in tow.

At first, with just the two of them, Julie had been tense. But, Millie's warm and informal manner had finally put her at ease.

Today, she planned to go into town to check on the preparation of the library wall. Fred had hired a local crew to fill in all the chinks and cracks, then to paint on a primer. After making sure that job was going well, she would talk to Nora Martindale, the librarian, to arrange a storage area for her painting supplies, once she got started on the mural. Then she would visit Abby Hawthorn at the museum, to pick up any research materials Abby might have for her.

The jeans on, Julie took one of her oversize T-shirts and slipped it over her head. She put on socks and her big shoes, then grabbed a handful of her unruly hair and fastened it at the nape with a rubber band. A touch of mascara and lipstick, and she was ready for the day.

Julie had come to Millie's full of worry and concern, caused mainly by the note she had received at the inn. But, so far, nothing upsetting had happened. Although several people had visited the house during the past few days, none had given Julie the slightest inkling they thought she was anyone other than the artist from Seattle who had been hired to paint the town murals.

Julie left her room and went downstairs, anticipating a

pleasant breakfast on the sun porch with her hostess. With Millie's interest in art, the two had something in common, and already they'd had several stimulating conversations. The smell of coffee wafted from the kitchen into the hallway. Julie's mouth watered in anticipation of her first cup.

As Julie reached the sun porch, the hall angled in a way that allowed her to glance into the room. She expected to see Millie, who was an early riser, seated at the table waiting for her. She was surprised to see not Millie, but a man sitting there. His back was to the door. He had broad shoulders and thick, dark hair curling at the nape. His head was bent over a newspaper.

Gregory.

Julie's heart raced and heat flooded her face. She had not seen or spoken to him since that awful scene outside the bank, when he had tried to date her, and she had refused. What was he doing here? She felt suddenly angry with him, as though he had invaded her territory.

Don't be ridiculous. This is his grandmother's home and he has every right to be here.

Unfortunately, the logic of that had no effect whatsoever on her tumultuous emotions.

She didn't want to go into the sun porch. Even her need for coffee couldn't push her in there. But what was the alternative? Perhaps she could return to her room and start downstairs again, and by that time he'd be gone.

While she was mulling that over, Hilda the cook bustled down the hall toward her. She held a steaming plate aloft in both hands. Her ruddy face beamed with a smile. "Saw you pass by the kitchen," she said to Julie. "And here's your breakfast, hot off the griddle. Eggs scrambled with bits of bacon, and whole wheat toast, just the way you like them."

"Why, thank you, Hilda," Julie said, with forced brightness. She wanted to add that she'd eat in the kitchen, or in the library, anywhere but the sun porch, but Hilda breezed by her and into the room in question. Julie had no recourse but to follow.

Hilda set the plate down on the table. Holding her breath, Julie slid onto the padded, cane-backed chair. The round table, covered with a yellow and white checkered cloth, and with a small vase of fresh yellow daisies in the center, seemed to have shrunk to half its size. She and Gregory were sitting close enough to reach out and touch each other. Not that they would want to, she hastened to remind herself.

"Good morning, Gran," Gregory said absently, his eyes focused on the newspaper. Julie read the title of it upside down: *The Wall Street Journal.*

"Good morning," she said.

At the sound of her voice, his head shot up. His jaw dropped. "What are you doing here?"

Julie unfolded her linen napkin and carefully spread it on her lap. "I've been here for several days. Your grandmother invited me to stay while I'm doing the murals. She thought I would be able to work better here than at the inn. I guess she didn't tell you."

"No, she didn't," he grumbled. "And I've been busy myself lately, and haven't been over here."

"I'm sorry if my being here is an intrusion," she said, keeping her voice calm while her insides were still on an emotional roller coaster. "I'd be happy to eat in the kitchen and give you some privacy with your grandmother."

"Never mind." He waved a hand, then picked up his newspaper, opened it up, and turned to another page. He carefully folded it again and went back to his reading.

Julie reached for the coffee carafe and poured herself a cup. But the heaviness in the pit of her stomach had spoiled

---

the pleasure of that first sip. He was giving her the cold shoulder. And no wonder. No man likes to be rejected, and that was exactly what she had done to Gregory.

If only he knew how she really felt, that she would love to go out with him. That she wanted to more than anything. That her heart ached furiously every time she thought about it. But, of course, she couldn't tell him her true feelings.

Julie studied him covertly while she sipped her coffee. She liked his neat, professional look. He wore dark brown slacks, a beige shirt, and a brown and blue striped tie. His suit jacket, neatly folded, hung over the back of a nearby chair.

He seemed to favor shades of brown, she decided, recalling the tan slacks and brown tie he'd worn that day at the bank. He was smart to choose those colors. They looked great with his light tan and his chocolate brown eyes.

Julie sighed. They had started out on the wrong foot because of the accident, had patched things up, and now were at odds again. Would she ever achieve a permanent truce with this man?

Gregory suddenly glanced up and caught her staring at him. Julie felt her face redden. She grabbed her fork and took a bite of eggs. Gregory frowned and went back to his reading.

Just when Julie felt she couldn't stand the silence any longer and was about to say something, anything, to break it, Millie arrived.

Like Julie, Millie was dressed casually in jeans and a T-shirt. But her shirt was a rich green color with a spray of bright sunflowers appliquéd to the front. Julie figured it cost about as much as half a dozen of the ones she herself wore.

Hilda followed on Millie's heels with her plate of food. Everyone said, "Good morning," and Millie settled in the seat between Gregory and Julie. Julie felt a little better with Millie as a buffer between them.

While they ate, Gregory stuck to his reading, leaving Millie and Julie to talk about the weather and the roses just beginning to bloom in the garden. Millie did not seem to mind his preoccupation, and centered her attention on Julie.

"What are your plans for today?" Millie asked after awhile.

"I thought I'd go into town and check on the prep for the library mural. Then see what Nora and Abby have turned up for me."

"Sounds like a day's work. Why don't you ride in with Gregory? He can pick you up this afternoon and bring you back."

Julie choked on a sip of coffee. "Oh, no, I—"

Millie's suggestion captured Gregory's attention. He shoved his newspaper aside and looked up, a frown creasing his brow.

"That's all right with you, isn't it?" Millie asked her grandson, either not noticing or just plain ignoring his apparent displeasure.

"Of course," Gregory ground out.

"It's really not necessary," Julie protested.

"Everything you have to do is all within walking distance," Millie said. "You don't have any need for your truck, do you?"

"Well, no," Julie conceded. Darn, why hadn't she thought of an excuse, some errand she had to run, for which she needed her own vehicle?

But she hadn't and now she was stuck.

"I guess I could ride with Gregory," she finished.

Julie dutifully accompanied Gregory, now wearing his suit jacket and carrying a black attaché case, out to his Jeep parked in the circular driveway. "Thanks for going along with your grandmother on the offer of a ride," she said. "But I, uh,

83

just remembered some errands I want to run, and I'll need my own transportation."

Gregory turned to look at her. His brown eyes bored into hers. "That really isn't true, is it?"

She looked down at the ground, unable to keep his intimidating gaze. "No. I'm just trying to spare both of us an uncomfortable situation."

"Don't worry about me; I'm just fine with it." He turned away and marched toward his Jeep. He opened the rider's side door and said to her, "Come on, get in."

Fearing that any more protest would create a scene that might be evident from the house, should anyone be watching, Julie walked toward the Jeep. She glanced at the back bumper and saw the dent. She winced. Being reminded of their accident only made the situation worse.

Sitting beside Gregory in the Jeep was even more uncomfortable than sitting with him at the breakfast table earlier. She could hardly breathe. And when she did, she was all too aware of his aftershave. The tangy aroma accented his already obvious masculinity. She noticed how strong-looking his hands were as he turned the key in the ignition and shifted the gears into reverse. How his muscular thigh was outlined under his slacks as he moved his foot from brake to gas pedal. Julie swallowed hard and turned toward the window.

Look at anything! Anything but him!

"So, how is the murals project going?" Gregory asked, once they had left the Linscott property and were on the main road to town.

As if he cares, Julie thought. However, she had to concede that he sounded amiable enough. Besides, any conversation was better than the uncomfortable silence she'd been enduring.

"I've got the sketches for the library and the theater nearly finished," she reported. "Actually, I'm doing three sketches for each, hoping that at least one of them will hit the mark with the committee."

"How long did you say you've been staying at Gran's? I guess I wasn't listening too carefully when you told me before."

"Since Tuesday."

"Hmmm, you must be all settled in by now."

"I'm really comfortable. The guestroom is lovely, and your grandmother is so hospitable. But I'm sorry if my being there upsets you."

"Quit apologizing. It isn't your fault. Gran is a very thoughtful person, and I'm not surprised she asked you to stay with her. And being there will make it easier to use her resources for your research."

"She's gone out of her way to make me comfortable," Julie said.

The trace of a smile—the first she'd seen today—tilted Gregory's lips. "Yeah, she's a pretty wonderful old gal. Are you finding some of our pictures helpful?"

"Oh, yes. I found several of both the library and the theater, in those albums you showed me that night at the reception. By the way, did you know the theater was built in the 1850s, and was first used as an opera house?"

"No kidding."

"Then in the 1920s it hosted a lot of vaudeville and other traveling shows that came to town. The building's gingerbread façade is pretty much just as it was originally, especially the part that makes the roof look peaked."

"And you're incorporating all that in your mural?"

"Not all of it, but some. I have to be selective."

"What about the one for the bank?"

Julie frowned. "Unfortunately, the subject of that is still to be decided. The committee meets Monday to pass on the sketches I've done so far. They'll probably discuss it then. I wish they would come to a decision, so that I could get started on the final drawings."

"Too bad there has to be such a hassle about it," Gregory said. "If it hadn't been for that Ben Gabriel, things would be a lot different now . . ."

Julie's stomach twisted into a knot. As if riding into town with Gregory weren't bad enough, now this troublesome— and dangerous—subject had to come up.

She looked out the window. They were winding down the hill toward town. She could see the lumberyard's gigantic crane shining in the sunlight, and the trees that filled the center of the city's park.

Gregory went on. "If Gabriel had been tried and punished for his crime, maybe the family wouldn't be quite so upset about it. But the coward ran away, and he was never caught. It's like unfinished business, you know?"

"Yes," Julie said. She knew she should have dropped the subject, but since it had been raised, she felt compelled to add, "But are you sure he was the murderer? Aren't alleged criminals supposed to be considered innocent until proven guilty?"

Gregory glanced at her and quirked an eyebrow. "Sorry, I don't put any stock in that old saying. There's never been any doubt in anyone's mind. Not in any Linscott's mind, anyway. He ran away. Why would he run if he wasn't guilty?"

"Well, maybe he thought going up against your family would be a futile effort. The Linscotts being so influential and powerful, and all. He might have just panicked and taken off."

"You sound like you're siding with him." Gregory's voice rose a notch.

"I'm not siding with anybody. I'm just . . . speculating," she finished lamely. Julie took a deep breath, hoping to ease the tension that had spread from her stomach up the back of her neck. She should have heeded her inner warning and dropped the subject. But no, she had to jump in with both feet.

"Sorry," he said. "I tend to get pretty upset about what happened to Cyrus, even though it was before I was born. I shouldn't jump on you. After all, it doesn't have anything to do with you, except that you got caught up in it because of the mural."

Julie didn't dare say anything to that. If she agreed with him, she would be lying. On the other hand, her disagreement might lead to uncomfortable questions.

Fortunately, the next turn in the road brought them to the town's business district. In just a couple more minutes, she would be away from him and on her own. She could hardly wait.

"Where do you want to be dropped off?" Gregory asked.

"The library will be fine. That's where Fred's crew is working today."

As they approached the library, Julie spotted a white van parked in front of the to-be-painted wall. The back doors were open, and paint cans, tools, and a paint-spattered white tarp were strewn over the ground. A man and a woman, both dressed in blue work shirts and white coveralls, stood atop scaffolding, plugging holes in the wall's cement surface. Another man did similar work at the ground level. Off to one side, a group of five or six teenagers lounged on the grass, watching the workers.

Gregory pointed to the teenagers. "There's one of the reasons I'm against your project."

"What do the murals have to do with them?" Julie asked,

unable to fathom what the relationship could be.

Gregory pulled the Jeep to the curb and took it out of gear. "They're some of our problem kids. No real home life, nothing to do, so they just hang around looking for trouble."

"They do look a bit tough," Julie conceded, studying the group.

The boys' hair was either dyed a vivid black or bleached to almost white and stood on end from excessive gel applications. Their tank tops showed off muscles and tattoos, and cigarettes dangled from their pouting lips.

The two girls both sported hair streaked with pink and lime green. Their faces were made up with dark eye shadow and bright-red lipstick. Their T-shirts looked two sizes too small and their cutoffs had ragged hems.

"They think they're tough," Gregory said. "But I think they just need some attention and care. I want to develop a recreation center for them. At least, that would give them a place to hang out."

"That sounds like a good idea." Julie still wondered what that had to do with her and the murals.

"It is, but your project took all the available money."

So that was what bugged him. Although she could see his side of it, she also refused to take the blame for something she had nothing to do with.

"I'm sorry," she told Gregory. "But, please, don't call it my project. It belongs to your grandmother and the others on her committee. She's the one you should be talking to, not me."

He shrugged. "I have talked to her. A lot. Didn't do any good."

"Even so, it's not my fault," she said, allowing annoyance to creep into her voice. The stress of their previous conversation was beginning to tell on Julie. Her patience for this new, also potentially troublesome topic had run out before the conversation got off the ground.

They sat there glaring at each other. Tension hung heavily in the air.

"We'd both better get to work." Julie turned away to unbuckle her seatbelt. "Thanks for the ride."

"Where shall I pick you up?"

She gave an inward sigh, reminded that she still had to deal with him later today. "I'll come to the bank."

He nodded curtly. "See you around five."

Julie hopped out of the Jeep. She watched Gregory wheel it around and roar off in the opposite direction. A sigh of relief escaped her lips. Being in his company made her a nervous wreck. She was constantly fearful she would say something that would give her away regarding her relationship to Ben Gabriel. Then, she'd had to defend herself on the subject of a center for the kids versus her murals project.

On top of all that was fighting her attraction to him. Whenever she first saw him, her heart would thud against her ribcage. And if they came within three feet of each other, she had trouble breathing. It was awful. What was she going to do?

Shoving all thoughts of the troublesome Gregory Linscott from her mind, Julie headed toward the crew. She was conscious that the teenagers had ceased talking among themselves and watched her. Before she reached the workers, one of the teens jumped up and approached her.

"What's goin' on here?" he asked.

Although he had bleached blond hair, a ring in one nostril of his pug nose, and a curl to his lips, at this close distance, Julie saw vulnerability in his pale-blue eyes. Also, he was younger than she had thought when studying the group earlier; he couldn't have been more than thirteen or fourteen.

"Hi," she said, keeping her voice friendly and casual. "We're going to paint a mural on the side of the building."

"A mural? What's that?"

"It's a painting on a wall that sometimes tells a story. This one will show the history of the library."

"Who cares about the *liberry's* history?" He gave a derisive snort, then turned around and stomped back to his cohorts.

Julie watched him for a minute, wondering if she should pursue him and offer more explanation, with the hope that he would then see the value of the project. But, no, perhaps it was better to just let him and his friends alone.

When the teen reached his friends, he leaned down and talked to them, gesturing back toward Julie and the building. They listened and once again regarded her curiously.

She turned away to approach the man working at the library's ground level. They introduced themselves. Hank Rawson looked to be in his fifties. Gray hair peeked from under his blue baseball cap, and ruddy cheeks indicated he was used to working in sunshine and fresh air.

Hank pointed to the teenagers, who were still sprawled under the trees. Although their expressions had returned to that of sullen boredom, Julie had the feeling they were watching every move she and the work crew made. "Better look out for them," Hank said. "They're trouble."

"They need something constructive to do," Julie said. "Aren't there jobs they could get during the summer?"

"They're not old enough to join the work force. Besides, would you hire somebody who looks like that?"

"I would have some reservations," Julie conceded, then changed the subject to ask Hank how their work was going.

"Fine, far as I know," he said. "We've never done exactly this kind of thing before, but Fred was good about explaining what to do. We should be finished before the day is over."

Julie watched long enough to assure herself that the crew did indeed know what they were doing. Then she headed around the building to the library's front door to find Nora Martindale.

As she passed them, she saw that the teens were huddled together, whispering and glancing now and then at the workers and the wall. Julie had a sudden tingle of apprehension that they were up to no good. She hoped she was wrong.

Chapter Eight

"Will this room do for storing your supplies?" Nora Martindale asked Julie. They stood in the library's dimly lit basement, peering into a room stacked with cardboard boxes, metal filing cabinets, and shelving boards.

Julie mentally measured the room's available floor space. "Yes, if you're sure you won't be needing it."

"I don't come down here often," Nora said. "The boxes contain records for our out-dated catalog system that we do have to dip into from time to time." She pointed to a wooden box with drawers the size of a three-by-five index card. "But as long as you leave me a path to them, that will be fine."

"I'll remember that," Julie said.

Nora shut the room's door. "Come on back upstairs. I have some photos for you."

Julie followed Nora up the narrow stairs. Confirming her first impression that the librarian favored bright colors, she noted that Nora's low-heeled shoes were the exact emerald green as were her slacks and the scarf encircling her mahogany-colored hair. Julie sighed. It must be nice to always be so coordinated with one's clothing.

Julie had to squint for a moment when they emerged from the dark basement and into the cheerful brightness of the library's main floor. Most of the light came from a stained-glass skylight, which cast a bright glow over bookshelves, computer terminals, and counters.

The library appeared to be a popular place. Julie looked around at all the people perusing the stacks, sitting in front of the computer terminals, or lounging in the arrangement of comfortable chairs. Beyond the chairs was a sunken area that she guessed was used for storytelling to children.

When they reached Nora's office, Nora pointed to a stack of papers and photos lying on the desk. "You can look through these now and see if there's anything you want. Or you can take the whole bunch with you."

"I'll look through them here," Julie said. "No sense in taking away stuff I don't need."

Nora nodded in agreement. "Feel free to stay here in my office. I'll be busy with children's story hour in a few minutes and won't be needing it."

"Thanks." Julie slung her tote over the back of Nora's swivel desk chair and prepared to sit down.

"Oh, there's something I wanted to show you." Nora riffled through the stack and pulled out a large colored photo. "This is a picture of all the original bank employees. This would be perfect for you to use—if Millie would only bend and allow all of the people to be shown." She slid the photo over so that Julie could see it.

Julie scanned the six men and two women, quickly spotting Cyrus Linscott, Harold Everton, and Joe Gordon. Then her gaze landed on the man at the end of the row. He had auburn hair—just like hers. And a small, turned-up nose—just like hers. Julie's breath stuck in her throat.

"That's Benjamin Gabriel, the man who's supposed to have murdered Cyrus." Nora's pink-nailed forefinger landed squarely on the man's face.

Julie swallowed hard. Her legs buckled under her and she landed in the swivel desk chair with a plop. Yes, it was her grandfather, and he did look like her. Or, rather, she looked like him. The similarity was more than she ever would have guessed, judging by what she recalled of the faded, worn-out old man she'd met in New York so long ago.

Although Julie had seen the resemblance right away, would anyone else? Would Nora? Self-consciously, Julie turned her face away, as she mumbled, "Oh, so that's the man the Linscotts hate so much."

"Yes," Nora said, her voice rising. "And I don't see why he can't be in the mural. After all, he was never proven to be the murderer. Just because he ran away right afterward doesn't automatically mean he killed Cyrus. But Millie is stubborn about having her way. I know she's our chairperson, but making decisions ought to be a more democratic process."

Nora talked on, but Julie barely listened. She was thinking that if she did use the picture, then surely someone, sometime, would notice the resemblance between her and Ben. For that reason alone, she hoped Millie did have her way, and the mural would not show this group of people. Surely there were other interesting subjects related to the bank that she could use.

Still, she dare not get involved by offering her opinion to Millie, or to any of the committee members. That would only draw more attention to her. She'd just have to wait and see what they finally worked out.

"Anyway," Nora said, "I thought this picture would be perfect for you to use. You could have each person doing something. Cyrus could be sitting at his roll-top desk, Harold and Joe could be talking to customers. The two women were the first tellers. They could be behind the tellers' cages."

"Thanks for the ideas," Julie said. "But I think I'll wait and see what the committee decides before I begin any work on it."

Nora looked about to say more on the subject, but, thankfully, just then, sounds of children's voices drifted in from the library's main room. Nora looked around. "Oh, there are the children for story hour." She reached to adjust the scarf around her hair and straighten the collar of her white blouse. "Got to go."

Julie breathed a sigh of relief as Nora strode from the room. She watched the toddlers and their adult caregivers follow Nora to the sunken storytelling area.

When they were out of sight, Julie dared to look at the picture again. She studied her grandfather. He had such an open, honest expression, not what one would expect of a murderer. But looks didn't always tell the tale, Julie reminded herself. Still, she just couldn't believe her grandfather had done such an awful thing. Sadness welled up inside her. *I wish I'd had the chance to know you better,* she whispered to the picture. Then she buried it back in the stack, and began to look through the other photos. It didn't take long to fill the accordion file Nora had provided her with relevant papers and photos.

"So, how's your work coming?" Abby Hawthorn asked Julie later that afternoon. They were sitting on white, wrought iron chairs in the museum's sunny courtyard. On the low table between them sat a pink porcelain tray, a matching teapot, two cups and saucers, and a plate of Abby's home-made, oatmeal raisin cookies. Behind them, a white trellis supported vines of scarlet roses in full bloom. The rich scent of the flowers filled the warm summer air.

"Pretty good," Julie replied. She told Abby about the sketches she had made for the library and the theater. "Nora gave me some more material today," she added. "I spent some time in her office looking it over and found some good photos."

Reminded of the troubling picture of her grandfather, Julie fell silent, gazing idly at the row of cedar trees marking the museum's property line. Beyond them was the beginning of the town's residential area, where children played on backyard swings, and flower gardens provided colorful contrast to the green lawns.

"You look worried," Abby remarked.

Julie jolted to her senses. "I do?"

"Thinking about the bank's mural, perhaps?" Abby asked, tilting her head. A light breeze lifted strands of her gray hair and curled them around her ears.

"It has been on my mind," Julie admitted.

"It's a shame the committee can't agree." A cloud swept over the sun, bringing a sudden chill to the air. Abby tugged her tan cardigan sweater closer over her chest, momentarily disrupting her glasses hanging on a chain around her neck. "We should've had that all decided before you came. But, of course, at that time, the bank wasn't to be included. That was Millie's idea, I guess because the bank is so important to the Linscott family."

"I'm sure it will all work out," Julie said. She didn't know what else to say about the touchy subject. She took a sip of her tea. She'd been pleased to find her favorite flavor, mint with a hint of tarragon, included in the selection Abby provided.

Abby nodded, and then turned the discussion to murals she'd seen on a cross-country trip to enjoy a New England fall. "It seemed as though every small town we passed through had them. They've become quite the rage. I'm glad I was on a tour bus and someone else was doing the driving. I got to see so much more that way."

As they chatted, Julie mused on how relaxed she felt with the museum's curator. While she liked all the committee members, Abby was the most down-to-earth. Her gray hair sat in a simple bun atop her head, her upturned nose and small mouth gave her face a childish look, despite her seventy-odd years. She looked like someone's grandmother, the kind who gave warm hugs and loving smiles. The kind who baked cookies and served them with warm milk when she took care of you. She was easy to talk to, as well, and Julie felt quite comfortable sitting here in the courtyard with her, enjoying a cup of tea and her delicious cookies.

Julie's thoughts made her wonder about Abby's family. She never spoke of any relatives. Nora talked about her son, a doctor in a Spokane clinic, of whom she was very proud. But Abby never mentioned husband or children. Or sisters or brothers, for that matter.

During the next lull in the conversation, Julie asked, "Does your family live in Cooperville?"

A shadow crossed Abby's plain face. "The only family I have is a younger sister who lives in Minnesota. We don't see each other very often."

"Your husband—"

"Luther passed away several years ago. We married late in life, and we had no children." Abby fingered her paper napkin. She looked as though she were about to say more, and Julie politely waited, raising her eyebrows to indicate her interest. Several moments passed before Abby went on.

"I was married before, when I was nineteen. His name was Edgar, and we had a son, Roger. Edgar and I divorced when Roger was three. Several years later, Roger died."

"How tragic," Julie said.

"It was. He was thrown by a horse. He was in a coma for several months, but finally passed away. It was a blessing, we were told, because, had he lived, he would have been brain damaged. It was hard on both Edgar and me. Edgar adored

97

his son, and was as good as a father could be."

"You were alone for quite awhile before marrying again, then?"

"Yes. There was a man in between, but . . ." Abby stopped to take a sip of tea. Again, Julie waited expectantly for her to finish. Abby put down her cup. She glanced at Julie, then bit her lip and looked away.

"I'm sorry," Julie said. "I didn't mean to bring up a painful subject. I was just curious, because you seem like the kind of person who would have a lot of family. And, well, you've never mentioned any relatives, so I thought I'd ask."

Abby offered a wan smile. "It's all right. I really don't mind talking about it. As I was saying, there was another man in between my first and second husband, but it didn't work out." Abby stopped talking again. She clutched her arms, as though she were cold, even though the cloud had passed and the sun shone brightly again. Her lower lip trembled. Clearly, she did mind talking about it.

Julie said, "You don't have to say any more. You've given me enough of an answer to my original question."

Abby drained her teacup, putting it back on the saucer. She looked at Julie, relief visible in her gray eyes. "Yes, perhaps we have been visiting long enough. If you're finished with your tea, let's go back inside. Like Nora, I, too, have some materials for you."

She settled Julie at the table in the Archives Room, where the Murals Committee met, then gave her a stack of bulging file folders. "I'm afraid this material isn't as organized as I would like it to be, but I'm sure you can find your way through it. You can make copies of anything you want to take with you."

A couple of hours later, Julie had added more to the accordion file she'd begun at the library. It was really bulging now.

She tied the string around it, so that the contents would not fall out.

At a quarter to five, Julie sat in the lobby of the Cooperville First National Bank, waiting for Gregory. When she'd arrived, she spotted him right away, talking to one of the tellers. When he saw her, he waved and pointed to the round wall clock, indicating it wasn't yet five. She nodded and took a seat on one of several overstuffed chairs near a large potted tree. Gregory had disappeared into his office.

Spying a coffee urn nearby, she got up and poured a cup, then sat back down again to drink it. After a couple moments of looking around without seeing anything of particular interest, Julie pulled from her tote the accordion file of material she'd collected from Nora and Abby, and riffled through it. There were pictures, notes, and drawings, a mishmash of memorabilia collected over the years. Her gaze lighted on the photo of the original bank employees, and lingered on the image of her grandfather. Julie sighed and stuffed the photo deep into the stack.

Ordinarily, such a storehouse of historical lore would have fascinated her, but just then, Gregory emerged from his office. He caught her eye and smiled, one corner of his mouth turning up more than the other in that characteristic way of his that had enchanted her from the very first. Her research material lay on her lap, all but forgotten. It seemed that whenever he was around, she couldn't look at anything else.

Covertly, she watched him lean over a woman employee's desk as they carried on a conversation. He seemed so absorbed that she felt certain he wouldn't catch her looking at him, so she let her gaze travel leisurely over his dark hair and broad shoulders. His face was partially hidden, but she could see a bit of high forehead and the strong line of his jaw, shadowed slightly by his beard line. He certainly was a handsome man.

The woman employee must have thought so, too, judging by the way she gazed at him with obvious admiration. They laughed, as if enjoying a good joke. Still smiling, Gregory accepted a proffered paper from the woman and headed back to his office.

Julie expected his good humor to be gone by the time he was ready to drive them home. However, a few minutes later when he came to collect her, the smile was still on his face.

"You must have had a good day," she commented as they headed for the back parking lot and his Jeep.

"I did." Gregory opened the door for her to climb in. "I feel very good about what I accomplished today."

"Did you grant lots of loans?" she pursued, when he had come around to his side and climbed behind the wheel.

Gregory shut his door. "No, I'm talking about something else. Oh, I did my job at the bank, as usual. And it went fine. I do like my work. But something else went right today. Very right."

"And that was?" She couldn't imagine what had made him so enthusiastic.

Gregory started the ignition and headed out of the lot. "Seeing those kids hanging around the library this morning spurred me to action. Remember, I told you I wanted to develop a recreation center for them, but that the money I hoped to get from the town council went for your murals?"

Julie nodded. She didn't like his referring to them as *her* murals, but now was not the time to complain about that. She wanted to hear what this was all about.

"Well, I decided not to give up," Gregory continued. "I

made a few phone calls, and what do you know, I found someone who will give us the use of a building."

"Really?"

He braked for a traffic light, turned, and studied her. She couldn't help but catch the enthusiasm radiating from his brown eyes. "Yep. It's on South Main. Until recently, Sims' Furniture was there, but they went out of business. The Kemper family owns the building—but, it's a long story; you're probably not interested."

"Yes, I am. Really."

The light changed and Gregory stepped on the gas pedal. "Okay, the Kempers own it, but Jake Kemper recently passed away. His widow—she's not hurting for money and has always had a charitable bent—said we could use the building, rent-free."

"Gregory, that's wonderful."

"Only thing is, we have to fix it up. But I figure we can find enough volunteers and donations for that. Even if it takes time, at least we have a place. That was the main thing."

"It sounds perfect."

"It is. There's room for a small basketball court, and a couple of other rooms for pool tables, and whatever. It has a kitchen, too, and we can fix snacks and such. Maybe even some meals now and then. There are offices for a director and a small staff."

He waved a hand. "It won't be just a place to play, though. I think I know where I can get some donated computers, and maybe someone to come in and teach the kids how to use them. I know they get some of that in school, but these are kids who don't seem to learn much in school. Maybe a different environment, where they aren't under pressure for grades, will work better."

"Great idea."

He shot her a triumphant look. "So, now I have my project to work on."

Good, Julie thought. Maybe that would take his attention from her project. Uh-oh, there she was, calling it *her* project, just as he did. But, aside from that, she thought the recreation center a wonderful and worthwhile idea. She even found herself wishing there were some way she could contribute to Gregory's about-to-become-a-reality dream.

"There's a center for kids near where I live in Seattle," she said. "It's also a place where people can post odd jobs they have that kids can do."

"I like that," Gregory said. He took a hand from the wheel long enough to pat his breast pocket. "I've got a pen here. I should be writing all this down."

"I'll make a list for you." Julie dug into her tote and pulled out her notebook and pencil.

"Put down what you just said, and also 'used computers,' " he directed. "What is that guy's name?" He snapped his fingers. "Oh, yeah, Barnes, something Barnes. Just put that down. The first name will come to me."

They both had several more ideas that Julie recorded. The minutes and miles slipped by and they left the town behind. Soon they were turning onto the tree-lined road leading to Millie's house.

"That's all I can think of, at the moment," Gregory said.

"Me, too."

Julie tore the list from her notebook and folded it in half. It had been fun helping him to plan his project. Nevertheless, she cautioned herself to not become too involved. She wouldn't be in Cooperville long enough to be of much help. Certainly she would not be there long enough to see the project through to completion. She would be long gone back to Seattle by then. Besides, she had her own work to do while she was here.

Gregory pulled the Jeep to a stop in front of Millie's house. "Here's your list," Julie said. As she handed it to him, their fingers touched. The air sizzled with electricity. She quickly pulled her hand away. Had he felt it, too? She didn't dare to look at him, even though she was dying to know whether or not he experienced the same startling jolt that she had.

"Thanks for being my secretary," he said, in a voice that sounded strangely thick.

"You're welcome. Thanks for the ride. I'll just hop out . . ."

Julie willed herself to move, but she was glued to the seat. The air between them grew so heavy with tension that she could hardly breathe. She finally turned to him and saw, with a little thrill of excitement—or was it alarm—that he had been studying her all the while. His eyes had darkened to a deep brown. The lids lowered as he focused on her mouth. His lips parted, expelling a breath that seemed to come from deep inside him.

Involuntarily, Julie reached up and touched her lips. They were dry. She pushed out her tongue, licked the dryness away. Gregory groaned. He leaned closer to her.

"Julie . . ."

No one had ever said her name quite like that before, with a mixture of wonder and surprise. Julie leaned in to meet him. She caught his scent, all male and musky. Intoxicating. Mesmerizing. She licked her lips again.

She and Gregory were mere inches apart now. He edged closer, narrowing the gap between them. His breath, warm and sweet, fanned her cheek. Julie's eyelids slid shut. He was going to kiss her—and she was going to let him.

Just then, Julie's tote, that had been on her lap since she'd retrieved the notebook and pencil, slid to the floor with a resounding thud. She and Gregory both jumped. Her eyes flew open. My goodness, she and Gregory were practically nose to nose. In another instant, she had no doubt their lips would have been locked together in a kiss.

What on earth had she been thinking? She didn't want to get involved with him like that. Correction: couldn't get involved.

She leaned forward and reached to retrieve her bag, saw that the accordion file had slipped out of it and was lying on the floor of the Jeep. "I, uh, I've got to go."

"What?" Gregory said, as though he had just come to his senses. "Oh, right, go." He sat up, and straightened his tie. "Julie—"

Julie put up a hand to stop him. "Please, don't say any more, Gregory. Let's just forget what happened."

"But nothing happened. . . . Did it?"

"Right. Nothing happened." Thoroughly flustered, she reached again for the tote, succeeded in pulling it back onto her lap. She twisted around, grabbed the door handle, and, although it was cold and hard to the touch, hung onto it as though it were her lifeline.

"Thanks again for the ride," she muttered.

"You're welcome. But, wait, I'm going in, too."

Julie's heart sank and she slumped against the door. Oh, no; she so much needed to be away from him, to put a vast distance between them, until she could get her emotions under control.

"Why?" she asked without turning around.

"Because I want to give Gran the news about my project. After all my complaining about it, I'm sure she'll be relieved to hear that it's underway at last."

"Oh."

There was nothing she could do about that. He had every right to go into his grandmother's home. She was only a guest there and had no say whatsoever about his comings and goings.

Gregory got out of the Jeep. Julie reached down to pick up her accordion file of papers, while he came around and opened the door for her. Juggling both the tote and the file, Julie stepped onto the Jeep's small running board.

"Here, let me take that." Gregory reached for the file.

Julie held it out, keeping her fingers as far away as possible from his. It was, after all, that jolt of physical contact when she gave him the note a few minutes ago that had started everything. Luckily, she'd come to her senses in time to prevent total disaster.

However, in trying to keep from touching him, her grip on the file was unsteady. Before she could make the transfer, the file fell to the ground.

Julie watched in horror as the string tied around it broke and papers and photos tumbled out. The light breeze immediately picked them up and began to scatter them around the lawn. "My papers!" she cried.

"We'll get them," Gregory said. "But let's get you out first." He grasped her elbow and helped her down. If there was a jolt that time, Julie was too preoccupied to feel it. She scrambled to retrieve the papers that were nearby, while Gregory ran to pick up those skittering around the corner of the house. Unfortunately, the breeze helped to disperse the material.

It took Julie a couple of minutes to recover all of the papers within her sight, a few of which had lodged in the holly bushes against the front of the house.

She returned to the Jeep to find Gregory, a fistful of papers in one hand, staring at a photograph he held in the other. Glancing over his shoulder, Julie saw that it was the picture of the original bank staff, the one Nora Martindale had given

105

her. The one that had Ben Gabriel in it.

Her stomach did a flip-flop. Would Gregory notice the resemblance between her and her grandfather?

Hearing her approach, he turned around. His brow was furrowed and his mouth was drawn into a tight line. *Uh-oh, this didn't look good.* Julie wished she could find a hole to crawl into.

Gregory's frown deepened. "I just noticed something about this picture," he said ominously.

Chapter Nine

Julie wanted to ignore Gregory's comment about the photo and to start walking toward the house.

However, she had the feeling that he wasn't going to drop the subject. She'd better inquire what the problem was and hope it didn't have anything to do with Ben Gabriel.

"That's one of the pictures Nora gave me this morning," she said, in as calm a voice as she could muster. "Is something wrong with it?" She held her breath as she waited for his answer.

"Not wrong, exactly; but incorrect."

"How so?"

"Well, I'm sure there were three women employees to start with. Two were tellers and one was a secretary. This picture shows only two women."

Was that all he was so upset about? Julie breathed a sigh of relief. "Nora didn't mention anyone was missing."

"That surprises me. Nora's such a stickler for details."

"That's been my impression of her, too. But maybe she doesn't know there were three women."

"Could be. Or maybe I'm wrong. I know what to do. I'll show this to Gran. She'll know if I'm right or not."

Julie wanted to grab the picture away from him but restrained herself to just reaching out and touching its edge with her fingertips. She hoped he would take the hint and yield it willingly.

"Let's not bother Millie with it right now," she said casually. "I'm concentrating on the other two murals, anyway. I won't be starting on the one for the bank until everyone comes to an agreement about what they want in it."

Gregory hesitated, still looking at the photo.

Please, please don't notice that I resemble Ben Gabriel, she silently pleaded.

He looked up at Julie. She held her breath again.

"Okay," he finally said, and turned the picture over to her. "It includes Ben Gabriel, anyway, and I'm sure she doesn't want to be reminded of him. We've heard enough of him lately."

"No, I'm sure she doesn't." Julie slipped the photo into the accordion file. She managed to tie what was left of the string attached to it. Her breath came easier now that she had control of the picture.

Inside the house, Julie quickly excused herself and escaped upstairs to her room, while Gregory went in search of his grandmother. Julie shut her door, tossed her tote and the accordion file onto the table, and sank onto the bed. Her hands were shaking and her face felt hot. That had been a close call. Too close.

Keeping her secret hidden became more stressful with each passing day. It affected her ability to concentrate on her work, and she feared the situation would get only worse, not better, as time went by.

Sure, today she had succeeded in keeping her grandfather's picture from Gregory, but how could she be sure more such pictures would not surface as the project went on? There were probably some in this very house, in the library credenza, with the Linscott memorabilia that Gregory had shown her on her first visit.

It tore Julie apart to be so deceptive. Since she arrived in

Cooperville, Millie had gone out of her way to help her. She'd opened her home, providing a lovely and comfortable atmosphere that would facilitate Julie's work.

Even Gregory had become easier to get along with.

But that in itself posed yet another problem. Look at what had almost happened today as they'd sat in his Jeep, in the driveway. She was certain he was going to kiss her. And, worse, she completely fell under his spell and was about to let him. That would have been a very bad move indeed.

Could she keep on resisting Gregory's charms? Could she keep her relationship to Ben a secret until all the murals were done and she was safely on her way back to Seattle?

She'd have to; that was all there was to it.

Julie put down her charcoal pencil, sat back, and studied her drawing. The arch of the doorway needed a little more curve. She picked up her eraser and gently rubbed out the line. Then, with a graceful sweep of her arm, drew a new one.

It was Saturday afternoon, a week after the near-disaster with Gregory. She'd put aside her work on the town murals to start on the one for Millie's shed. She sat on a grassy hillock under the shade of a large, gnarly maple, where she had a good view of the shed and of the wall to be painted. Beyond the shed lay a meadow, where wildflowers waved in the light breeze, sending their sweet scent in her direction.

She had decided to make the mural a *trompe l'œil*, which meant, "trick of the eye." A *trompe l'œil* fooled the viewer into thinking that the mural was reality.

In this case, she would make the shed wall look like the wall of a stable. A horse would peer from the open top half of a door. Up above, birds would perch on a windowsill. The realistic rendering would convince viewers that they could walk right over and pet the horse, and that the birds might, at any time burst into song.

When she'd told Millie of her idea, the woman clapped her hands in delight. "I love it," she said. "I used to have a favorite horse named Misty. She had the loveliest butterscotch-colored coat and a long, pale yellow mane and tail. Maybe the horse in the stable could be like her?"

"Sure," Julie said. "Just give me a picture of Misty and I'll do my best to create her likeness."

She was confident she could pull off the illusion. She'd helped her mentor, Gerard Bronson, paint several *trompe l'œil* murals around Seattle and had learned the techniques for making them successful. The actual painting would not be done until after the downtown building murals were finished, but she figured she could get a start on the design during her spare time.

Julie finished outlining and shading the stable door, then began work on the window where the birds would perch. She'd have to decide what kind of birds they would be. She'd ask Millie; she might have a preference.

Above her, the sun shone through the leaves of the tree, warming her head and shoulders. From the depths of the surrounding forest, birds sang to one another, and from the house drifted sounds of Millie's favorite classical music. She was relaxing this afternoon with a new book she'd borrowed from the library. Julie felt relaxed, too; even though she was working. Her work was also her relaxation. She could think of no better way to spend such a pleasant Saturday afternoon.

The crackling of branches startled her. She twisted her head around. There stood Gregory, dressed casually in jeans and a blue T-shirt. The short sleeves showed off his muscular arms.

"Oh!" she exclaimed. "How long have you been here?"

"Only a few minutes. I wasn't spying on you, either. You

were so deep into your drawing that I didn't want to disturb you. But I am curious about what you're doing."

"I'm sketching a mural your grandmother wants me to paint on the shed."

He nodded. "She told me about it."

"And that it's to be a *trompe l'œil?*"

"Yes. I saw some of those when I was on vacation in Europe last summer. And a friend's home on Long Island has the entire dining room wall a *trompe l'œil*. It's a rain forest with all sorts of exotic birds and animals wandering around, peeking from behind bright foliage. It was very impressive."

"They can be."

Gregory sat down beside her. Her breath caught in her throat at his sudden nearness. In the last week, they'd both kept their distance from each other. She'd made it a point to drive herself into town when the occasion warranted, and had avoided the bank, as well. She'd seen him at Millie's a few times, but other people had always been present. They'd both been polite to each other, but neither had sought the other out.

Just when she'd decided he wasn't going to pose a problem anymore, here he was, so close she could reach out and touch his bare arm. So close she could savor his masculine scent, a combination of aftershave and his own special essence. So close she could finger the lock of dark brown hair that fell casually over his forehead.

"It looks like a door with a window above it," Gregory said.

"What?" Julie struggled to regain her senses.

"Your drawing. I'm trying to figure it out."

"Oh, it is a door. A stable door. There will be a horse inside and birds on the windowsill." She slipped a photograph from under her drawing pad and handed it to him. Re-

111

membering how undone she came when they touched each other, she carefully kept her fingers from brushing his.

Gregory smiled at the photo. "Ah, Misty. I remember her. Gran's favorite. I used to ride her, too. She was a sweet old thing."

"Your grandmother thought it would be nice to have the horse as part of the mural."

"Good idea." He returned the photo. "Since you've been here, I've realized that murals are more than idle pictures on a wall."

"Really?"

Pleased by his comment, she met his gaze, and they exchanged smiles. Julie felt something unspoken pass between them, though neither said anything aloud. The sense of communication without words or without physical contact was new to her. A little thrill of excitement skittered along her spine.

Apprehension followed close on the heels of the excitement, however. An inner voice warned, *Careful, Julie.*

She broke eye contact and doodled on the edge of her drawing. Doodling usually relaxed her, but this time, her fingers tensed up. She gave it up and tossed down the pencil. "I take it you're here visiting your grandmother."

"More or less," he replied vaguely. "There's a dinner party to attend this evening. A command performance, although that makes it sound as though I don't enjoy Gran's parties, and I do."

"A dinner party? Millie said something about company, but a party sounds so formal."

He waved a hand. "Don't worry about it. That's what she always calls it when she invites people for a meal. Anyway, I came over to see if she needed my help for anything. She didn't. She happened to mention you were out here

112

sketching, so I thought I'd come by and see what you were doing."

"I see."

"It's a great day," he went on. "If you're ready for a break, why don't we take a walk through the meadow? I am your official tour guide, you know." He grinned and quirked an eyebrow. "Or have you explored the grounds on your own?"

Take a walk with Gregory? Julie's heart thudded. "No, I haven't done much exploring. Not beyond this shed, as a matter of fact."

"So, how about it?"

A walk with Gregory would be dangerous. Tell him you need to keep working on your drawing.

Come on, another voice argued, *you can handle being with him. He's Millie's grandson; you can't afford to be rude to him. You've got to learn to associate with him and not let it bother your emotions.*

"I am stiff from sitting here so long." She shifted her legs from their cramped, tucked-up-under-her position.

"Then a walk is just what you need."

Julie closed the cover on her drawing pad and put her pencils and erasers away in their plastic pouch.

"You can leave those in the shed," Gregory said. "They'll be okay there."

He rose and held out his hand to her. Uh-oh, here was the first test of her new resolve to treat him objectively. She could have easily stood on her own, but ignoring his gesture seemed rude. She placed her hand in his and let him assist her.

Once upright, she teetered on a lumpy bit of earth and lost her balance. She would have fallen against him, had she not quickly thrust a hand against his chest.

Her test had just taken a very difficult turn. With anyone else, she would hardly have noticed the physical contact, but with Gregory, every touch carried with it an awareness that left her just short of stunned. She jerked her hand away.

"Sorry," she managed to say. "I'm not usually so clumsy."

"No problem."

She glanced at him. His composed features indicated he hadn't been as affected by their contact as she had. Okay, if he could keep his control, so could she. By the time they dropped off her sketching materials in the shed, Julie felt calm and cool.

They left the shed and followed a path along the grove of maple trees that eventually opened out to the meadow.

"This is where the horses grazed when Al was here," he commented.

"Al?"

"Albert Jensen. He was Grandmother's second husband."

"I've never heard her mention him," Julie said.

"I think he's been more or less forgotten. She married him after Cyrus had been gone for about eight years. Al was okay, but he never fit in very well with the rest of the family. He had been a rancher and that was all he was interested in. Banking bored him. So, he kept horses and raised a little hay and even a few cows."

"Cows? Somehow, I can't see Millie milking cows."

Gregory laughed. "You're right about that. Horses were okay; she enjoyed riding. But I don't think she ever went near the cows. But Al was pleasant enough, and he thought the world of her. They lasted only a couple of years together, and then one day decided to go their separate ways. Last I heard, Al was living on a little farm in Idaho."

"And she never married again?"

Gregory held aside a low growing tree branch to allow them to pass. "No, that was it for her. I think part of the problem with Al was that Gran never got over Cyrus's

114

death. He was her one true love."

Julie's stomach lurched at the mention of Cyrus. She hoped Gregory wouldn't keep talking about his grandfather, because it always upset both of them.

Thankfully, he said nothing more about Cyrus, and continued to point out more sights instead. "There was a stable and a barn over there, but they've long since been torn down. The shed you're painting the mural on is from Al's era, too. He's the one who built it; but it was useful, so it didn't get demolished."

Julie looked around at countryside that seemed to stretch to forever. "How many acres does the estate include?"

"Nearly a hundred."

"That's a lot," she said, impressed that any one person would own so much land.

"Not around here. But I guess it would seem so to a city woman like you." His brown eyes glinted with a hint of teasing.

She grinned in return. "Yeah, the widest open spaces I ever see, besides the waters of Puget Sound, are a few city parks. My mother's house is on a third of an acre, which is considered a large lot in Seattle."

"So, how does it feel to be out here in the country?"

"I like it. It's a nice change."

While they had been talking, Gregory led them along a well-worn path that bordered the meadow. Fence posts and barbed wire peeked here and there through the overgrowth. Wild roses and hollyhocks joined dandelions and daisies, giving the grasses even more color than before. Scents of pine and fir drifted from the surrounding woods, while in the distance, purple hills blended with a deep blue sky.

The path led them to a wooden bridge arching over a bubbling stream. They leaned against the railing and stared down into the water. It ran along like liquid silver, cascading over an occasional outcropping of rock.

"The water looks so clear," she said.

"It is," Gregory said. "No pollution to speak of out here."

"Where does this stream go?"

"I'm not sure, but I'd be willing to bet it joins up eventually with the Columbia River. Once when I was a kid, my father and I followed it up north, to see where it went. But we could only go a few miles before the terrain got too rough. In the spring, it's really pretty with all the wild crocuses blooming along the shore. And in the fall, when the leaves turn, their reflections color the water."

Julie tried to imagine what it would be like to live where nature so vividly marked the passing of the seasons. True, there was some of that in the city; but crocuses usually grew in pots or small garden plots, rather than by streams; and turning leaves didn't reflect very well on pavement and asphalt.

The path veered away from the meadow and into the woods. Fallen trees covered with moss and lichen were scattered throughout with fir, pine, and hemlock towering over them. Leafy ferns and snaky vines grew alongside the trail. Occasionally, wild flowers she didn't know the names of poked their heads through the underbrush.

"Does this lead any place in particular?" she asked, enjoying herself, but curious about their destination.

"You'll see in a couple of minutes," Gregory said. "I did have a destination in mind, although we took a roundabout way getting to it."

As the trees thinned, a two-story, older home came into view. A motley-looking plot of grass surrounded the building. A few flowers bordered it, as though someone had half-heartedly started a garden.

"This is my place," Gregory said, just as she noticed the white Jeep sitting in the driveway. She heard a note of pride in his voice.

"Oh, that's right. I remember Millie telling me you live nearby."

"This was part of the original property Millie and Cyrus owned," Gregory explained. "The house was built by the owner before them, in the 1920s. I bought it last year, when—" He stopped and frowned.

She waited for him to finish, but instead, he said, "Anyway, come on inside. I haven't finished fixing it up, but it's presentable."

It was more than presentable. As they mounted the front porch, Julie noticed that the front door had a lovely oval panel of stained glass, and there were matching stained-glass panels above wooden casement windows. Inside, the hardwood floors gleamed. The living room was comfortably furnished in a style befitting its male inhabitant, with a leather sofa, chairs, bookcases, TV, and stereo system.

But it was the kitchen that really drew her attention. "Oh, I love it," she said, running her hand over the black and white tiled counters and the large cupboards with leaded-glass doors.

"It's all original stuff," Gregory said. "The tile's kind of a pain to keep clean, though."

"I bet you don't do it," she teased.

"You're right; I have a great cleaning lady. Say, as long as we're in the kitchen, how about something to drink?"

Whetting her thirst after their walk through the meadow and woods sounded good. "Okay, what have you got?"

He opened the refrigerator and peered inside. "Hmmm, maybe I should have looked before speaking." He pointed to shelves that were mostly empty. "Wait, there are a couple cans of soda. Or I could make coffee." He slanted her a glance.

"Soda is fine."

Gregory took out the cans and popped them open. He pulled two glasses from the cupboard and filled them. He brought the glasses to where Julie leaned against one of the counters. He held out one and stepped closer to her. Their gazes met. He was so near she could see little flecks of amber in his brown eyes.

"Julie?" He said her name part in question, part in wonder.

She had trouble breathing. "I, uh," she managed to mumble, but had no idea what she wanted to say. Gregory's gaze lingered on her mouth. Time stopped.

Without saying a word, yet with an intense look that clearly spelled out his intentions, Gregory put the glasses down on the counter, one on either side of her, and took her into his arms.

Words of protest sprang to her lips and quickly died there as he pulled her against his chest. She leaned into him, feeling a delicious warmth spread through her, feeling his heart beating steadily under the fabric of his shirt.

Gregory wound his fingers around the tendrils of hair that hung beside her ear. "I've wanted to touch your hair for a long time," he whispered. "It's so silky, just like I imagined it would be."

"It's always such a mess."

"Don't say that. It's beautiful."

He released her hair and feathered his fingers across her cheek, setting off little tremors along her nerve endings. His touch was so warm and gentle, that for a moment, she wanted to cry.

"I've wanted to do this, too." Gregory cupped her chin,

lifted her face, and closed his mouth ever so gently over hers.

The fusion of their lips left Julie weak-kneed. It was everything she thought it would be, and more. She put her arms around his neck and kissed him back. She let her fingers drift up his nape, into thick waves of his hair.

He tightened his hold on her, his fingers pressing firmly into the small of her back, then moving down to meet the curve of her hips. His mouth opened slightly; then he hesitated, as though waiting for her response. She opened her mouth, let his tongue glide across her lower lip then slip inside to mingle with her own tongue.

It was a wonderful kiss. Julie had no idea how long it went on. It could have been seconds. Or minutes. She lost all sense of time, and of place. They could have been floating on a cloud above the mountains, for all she knew.

Instinctively, they both drew away at the same time. Gregory gazed into her eyes. "Nice," he said, a soft smile tilting one corner of his mouth.

"But, we shouldn't—" she began, the protest that had arisen earlier having a voice at last.

He gently laid a finger over her lips. "Come on, now; I liked it. You liked it."

"Maybe so, but—"

"Don't spoil it with regrets or analysis. Relax." Gregory stroked her hair, the nape of her neck, her back. But tension kept her rigid.

Finally, he said, "Okay, maybe it'd help to sit down. Let's take our drinks out to the porch."

Julie nodded. "That sounds like a good idea."

Chapter Ten

On the porch, Julie surveyed the seating arrangement: a wooden, cushion-covered swing hanging by chains from the ceiling, two straight chairs, a rocker, and a white wicker table. The swing looked inviting; but if she sat there, Gregory would probably sit beside her, and she needed to put some distance between them. Julie chose the rocker. It, too, was cushioned on the seat and the back, and she sank into it gratefully.

Gregory sat in one of the straight chairs across from her. When he stretched out his legs, one foot almost touched hers. She wished she could stop thinking about Gregory and how his nearness affected her. The kiss certainly had affected her. Her lips still tingled from it. Not even sips of the cool soda could banish the scorching memory of his mouth on hers.

Striving to keep her mind in the present, and to not think about what repercussions the kiss might have on their future relationship, she gazed at the yard. White painted rocks lined an asphalt driveway that snaked out of view around a curve. A giant maple tree stood near the house, its leaf-laden limbs swaying in a soft breeze. Beyond the tree, almost out of sight, sat a detached garage that appeared newer than the house itself. Probably a later addition, she mused.

Following her gaze, Gregory said, "I was going to plant a garden, but never got around to it. Maybe next spring."

Seizing on that as a safe, neutral topic, she asked, "What will you plant?"

He shrugged. "I don't know. Peas, corn, some lettuce. It just seems the thing to do when I have all this land. There's a stable out back with a couple of horses, too." He turned to look at her as though an idea had just struck him. "Do you ride?"

"I have before, but not recently. Not much chance for that in the city."

He nodded. "I was thinking that we could take a ride today, but there isn't enough time. We'll take a rain check on it."

She didn't want to commit herself to any future dates with him. She had a lot of serious thinking to do before she agreed to horseback riding or anything else—if ever. "How long have you lived here?" she said, hoping to change the subject.

Gregory took a sip of his soda. "Almost a year."

"It's a nice place."

He nodded. "I like it okay, even though it's far from town. The truth is, though, I didn't plan on living here alone." He glanced away, then back at her. "I might as well tell you," he said with a shrug. "I bought the place from Millie when I was thinking about getting married."

"Oh."

The thought of someone else in Gregory's life sent a sharp pain shooting through Julie's heart. *Don't be silly. His past love life means nothing to you.* Still, she was curious to hear the story, and was glad when he went on.

"Her name was Marlys Stuart. She lived in Spokane. She came to Cooperville a couple of summers ago to work at Jensen Realty. Since the realty office is right across the street from the bank, it was easy for us to become acquainted."

"I see," Julie said.

"I dated her and eventually introduced her to the rest of

the family. She told us she came from a socially prominent family back East, where her father was a big land developer. She named several prestigious schools she'd attended. It was all very impressive." He paused and ran his thumb around the rim of his glass. "We got serious."

The ensuing silence lasted so long that she finally prompted, "So what happened?"

"Turned out what she told us was all a bunch of lies."

"Lies?" A sinking feeling hit Julie in the pit of her stomach. "How did you find out?"

"From an old boyfriend of hers. He'd heard she was here and came to look her up. He soon learned what she'd told us and—out of revenge, I guess—informed me that none of it was true. I told Millie. She had Marlys investigated and discovered that the boyfriend was right. Marlys wasn't who she said she was at all. She came from Los Angeles, where her parents owned a small, neighborhood grocery store."

"So you broke off the engagement."

"You bet I did," he said emphatically. "It didn't really matter to me whether she came from a prominent family or not. I guess she made up the story because she felt she needed to impress us. But, if she'd make up stories about that, she might lie about other things, too. I wouldn't have been able to trust her."

"I see your point," she said.

He shook his head. "That experience really made me aware of how important honesty is in a relationship. Honesty has always been a big thing to the Linscotts, anyway. After Marlys, it became more important than ever. I could never get involved with someone who lies."

Julie's face grew hot. "Don't you think there are circumstances when it's okay to lie? Well, not lie, exactly, but withhold the truth—for a very good reason, perhaps?"

Gregory shook his head. "No, I don't think it's okay under any circumstances."

She glanced away, not trusting herself to say anything more. Her heart pounded, her throat had dried up. She took a sip of soda, but it did little good.

Gregory remained thoughtful for a few more moments, then his expression brightened. "But, hey, let's forget about her. A moment ago, I was trying to picture what she looked like, and I couldn't. The only face I could see in my mind's eye was . . . yours." Brown eyes glittering, Gregory leaned forward and took her hand. "Julie—"

Julie held her breath, sorely tempted to give in to her growing feelings for Gregory. However, she knew that, especially in light of what he had just told her, weakening now would lead straight to disaster.

Gregory tightened his grip and drew her forward. "You're too far away from me over there. Let's sit on the swing."

If they moved to the swing, chances were they'd be in each another's arms again sharing more kisses. Although at this moment, she wanted that more than anything, she knew what she had to do.

Heartsick, she took a deep breath. "I don't think so, Gregory. We'd better be getting back to Millie's. We don't want to be late for the dinner party."

Gregory turned his wrist over to look at his watch. "Five already? Oh, well, nobody arrives till about six. And that's allowing an hour for cocktails. Dinner is actually served at seven."

"I need time to change clothes."

"You look great just the way you are."

"In jeans and T-shirt? No, your grandmother and her company deserve better than this."

Gregory gave her a pained look, then smiled. "Okay,

you're right. Give me a couple of minutes to put on something more presentable myself, and then we'll both go over to Gran's together." He rose, leaned down, and planted a quick kiss on her forehead. Then he picked up their glasses and headed into the house.

It occurred to Julie that she could insist on returning to Millie's by herself. But why, really? She and Gregory had shared a kiss, finally; a hot, passionate kiss that sent her world tilting on its axis. But now things between them seemed more or less back to the way they were. They were still speaking to each other, carrying on a conversation, albeit one that had given her even more reason to keep her secret regarding her relationship to Ben Gabriel.

She sighed and settled deeper in the rocker, resigned to wait for Gregory.

He finally appeared, looking all too gorgeous in dark gray slacks and a lighter gray silk shirt. That color looked almost as good on him as brown shades did.

They went back to Millie's following the road, rather than retracing their steps through the woods. As they walked along, Julie's thoughts turned to the upcoming evening.

"Do you know who's coming to dinner tonight?" she asked.

"Aunt Violet and Cousin Helen. You met them at the reception." She nodded. Gregory continued. "Gran's pal, Lila Jakowski. Oh, and Joe Gordon. You remember him?"

Her heart sank at that news. Of course, she remembered Joe, Cyrus's old business partner. He was the one who'd said she reminded him of someone. The thought of being under Joe's fierce scrutiny again twisted her stomach into a knot. She wished there were some way she could get out of making an appearance, but that was unlikely.

Then an idea that had been hovering deep within her mind

finally rose to consciousness.

Maybe you should come clean and tell Gregory the truth. Just get it out in the open and take the consequences. Wouldn't that be better than all this stress every time you're together?

She slanted him a glance. He seemed so happy, his mouth tipped up in a smile. They'd had a really pleasant time today, overall. They'd shared a wonderful kiss. Did she want to risk spoiling that?

Tell him.

Julie cleared her throat, then began, "Gregory—"

"What?"

"I, uh, about my being here in Cooperville—"

Before she could continue, he took her hand and tucked it under his arm. "You know," he said, "I am really glad you came to Cooperville, and that we're getting to know each other. Aren't you?"

Julie swallowed hard and looked away. "Yes, I'm glad, too."

"Now, what were you going to say?"

Her courage, not terribly strong to begin with, vanished like a puff of smoke.

"N-nothing," she said. "Nothing important."

"Do have some more mashed potatoes, Gregory." Grandmother held out the bowl to him.

Gregory took it and dutifully added a spoonful to the fried chicken drumstick and minted peas already on his plate. Normally, he ate heartily, but tonight he was too preoccupied to eat. Julie sat directly across from him, and all he wanted to do was gaze at her.

A wide blue band held her auburn hair away from her face, showing off her creamy complexion. She wore the same navy skirt she'd worn to the party Gran had for her. He liked that skirt, because it showed off her gorgeous legs. They were hidden under the table now, of course, but he'd filled his gaze with their loveliness earlier.

Her light-blue blouse was one he hadn't seen before. It was plain except for a narrow strip of lace around the neckline. He liked her in simple clothes. He liked her with just a touch of makeup. *Let's face it, you like her, period.*

He caught her eye as she lifted a forkful of fried chicken to her mouth. He winked. She smiled back. The exchange made him feel warm inside, like they were sharing secrets.

He had been worried that sharing that heated kiss at his place might have upset her. Apparently, it hadn't. She had responded to him more than he'd ever dreamed she would. Encouraged, he planned to forget her earlier rejection and resume pursuing her.

He wished he hadn't told her about Marlys, though. Not that he wouldn't have eventually; but she'd seemed awfully quiet after that. He certainly didn't want her to think he wasn't ready for someone new in his life.

He was.

He was ready for her.

Tomorrow, he would bring the horses over and take her riding. They would follow the meadow trail into the foothills—

"Gregory, are you with us?" Hearing his name jolted Gregory back to the present. The speaker was Cousin Helen. She was peering at him from around Aunt Violet, who sat next to him. Helen's pale blond hair was slicked back in a tight chignon that made her appear older and more sophisticated than usual.

"Of course," Gregory replied. "Just busy eating." To prove it, he cut another slice from his chicken drumstick.

"Well, then, answer my question," Helen said.

126

"Sorry, I guess I was daydreaming a little." He glanced at Julie, but she was sipping from her wineglass. He turned back to Helen. "What was your question?"

"I want to know if you'll go with Tom and me and Daria to Spokane to see a play."

"Daria?"

"You remember her, my old college roommate? You met her last Christmas when she was here."

"Hmmm." Gregory's mind drew a blank.

"She had that cute little red sports car you liked."

A light bulb went on in his head. "Oh, right. The Porsche." What a sweet little car that had been. Riding in it had almost made him want to go out and buy one for himself.

"I knew you'd remember the car, at least." Helen's comment set off a titter of laughter around the table.

"Anyway," his cousin went on, "the play is called *The Charmer* and has really good reviews. It's playing at that funky old theater in the historical district."

"My daughter and I saw it," Lila Jakowski said, flashing a hand laden with several rings set with turquoise stones. "It's funny, Gregory; you'll like it."

Gregory turned to his grandmother's friend. Lila Jakowski was a small woman, compared to Millie's stately height, anyway. She dyed her hair strawberry blond and had a penchant for Navajo jewelry that she acquired during winters spent in Arizona. She lived in the neighboring town of Wilton; but since her husband had passed away, she'd been spending a lot of time here in Cooperville. Gregory wouldn't be surprised if she would someday announce she was moving here. That was all right with him; he liked her and thought she made good company for Millie.

"I trust your judgment, Lila," Gregory said, "but I don't know . . . I'm going to be pretty busy in the coming days." He couldn't help glancing at Julie as he spoke. This time, she met his gaze. Her eyes widened; then she looked quickly down at her plate. She wasn't eating much, either, he noticed. Had she been busy thinking about him, too?

"Oh, come on," Helen said, a complaining note creeping into her voice. "You've always had time for my friends. What's keeping you so busy?"

"Gregory's got a new project," his grandmother put in from her place at the head of the table. "He's putting together a center for teens. You all know where Sims' Furniture was?" Everyone nodded. "Well, the owner of the building is allowing Gregory to use it for his center, rent-free."

Gregory silently thanked his grandmother for rescuing him. "Right," he said. Encouraged by everyone's interested look, he related the details.

"Harold will be so proud of you," Aunt Violet said. "He was always interested in helping kids. Remember how he used to have those big Halloween parties for them? And he'd disappear and return dressed up as the Devil. Most of the kids never caught on and were sure he was the real thing. It was great fun. Anyway, I'll be sure to tell him about your project, Gregory."

"How is Harold?" Millie asked.

Violet's mouth turned down. "Not good. The doctors say he's continuing to go downhill. Plus, his spirits are low. It's hard to interest him in anything."

"I saw him yesterday," Joe said. "And I agree. He seemed more depressed than ever."

"Would more visitors help?" Gregory asked. "I could go up there tomorrow." He could do that, he decided, and still have time for a horseback ride with Julie.

"That would be good of you," Aunt Violet said. She looked around the table. "You've all been so wonderful, so supportive."

The conversation jumped from topic to topic until Gregory's grandmother mentioned she'd asked Julie to paint a mural on the shed. "Tell everyone your idea," she said to Julie.

Gregory watched Julie's face light up as she explained her stable and horse illusion. She certainly liked her work. He tore his gaze away to check the others' reactions. Everyone had a pleasant, interested look, except Joe, who was frowning.

Grandmother noticed Joe's look, too, for when Julie finished, she said, "Joe, you look as though you don't approve. I know you thought I should have torn the shed down long ago, but—"

"It's not that." Joe absently ran a hand along the side of his thinning gray hair. "It's just that I'm still wondering why Julie looks so darn familiar."

So that's it, Gregory thought. Well, that was Joe. Once he had a problem, he didn't rest until it was solved. Gregory's father used to say that Joe was like a bulldog gnawing away at a bone until the thing just splintered into pieces.

"Still can't figure it out, eh?" Gregory said. Then he glanced at Julie and was shocked at how stricken she looked. Why? Did she have some deep, dark past to protect? He almost laughed aloud at that. Julie was the most open and honest person he could think of. He tried to catch her eye and give her a reassuring look, but she refused to glance his way.

"People used to say I reminded them of Grace Kelly," Lila said. "You know, the movie star who married that prince and then years later died in a tragic car accident?"

"Oh, yes," Helen said. "I've watched some of her movies on DVD." She cocked her head at Lila and looked puzzled. "I'm not sure about a resemblance, though . . ."

Lila said defensively, "Of course, that was when I was a

good deal younger. No one has said that lately."

"You've got her cheekbones," Aunt Violet said helpfully. "And when you were younger your hair was the same blond color as hers."

Lila sighed. "Too bad I couldn't have married a prince, like she did."

Millie took a sip of wine, then said, "So, Joe, maybe it's a movie star Julie reminds you of."

Joe shook his head. "Haven't been to the movies in years. Always considered them a waste of time."

Gregory felt a sudden impulse to protect Julie, even though he had no idea why she appeared so distressed. "Give it a rest, Joe," he said sharply. "It isn't important."

"Maybe, maybe not." Joe met Gregory's gaze with challenging eyes. Yep, he was like a dog with a bone, all right.

Joe looked down the table at Julie again. "It'll come to me," he said. "Eventually."

The following day, Julie drove along the freeway in her red truck, pushing the speed limit. She was about ten miles out of Cooperville, well into farm country. On both sides of the road were farms with either wheat fields or cows and horses grazing in grassy meadows. The purple mountains in the distance provided a colorful backdrop to the pastoral scenes.

But Julie hardly noticed the picturesque landscape. She was too busy coping with her inner turmoil.

Today, instead of working on her sketches, as she had planned, she'd desperately needed to get away from the Linscott estate. Yesterday had been a roller coaster of emotions that left her unable to concentrate. On the walk with Gregory, she had been happy and exhilarated. She was glad to share his company and get along so well with him.

At his house, the kiss had catapulted her into a new state of delirious joy. Afterward, hearing about Marlys Stuart's deception sent her spirits plummeting. Finally, enduring Joe Gordon's relentless scrutiny at dinner wound her nerves so tightly she wanted to scream.

After the dinner party, she had escaped to her room, pleading a headache. But, in reality, a cold fear had settled over her. She had restlessly paced her room, mulling over the troublesome situation. What if Joe finally figured out that she resembled her grandfather and told the Linscotts? Maybe he already had and was the one who'd sent her the note. Maybe he was biding his time for some other reason.

If he hadn't sent the note, then there was another person who knew of her relationship to Ben. What if that person told on her? Then what?

She'd be fired. And humiliated, disgraced, and shamed.

Did she want to wait around for that to happen? She could, right now, just keep on driving and be home to her apartment in Seattle by tomorrow. She could have Audra DeSoto, when she arrived next week, gather up her belongings and send them to her. Audra could take over the project.

But could Audra manage the project? She was a competent painter and a good friend, but she'd never headed up a job of this magnitude. For that matter, neither had Julie. That's why the success of it was so vital to her.

What to do? The problem gnawed relentlessly at her.

Spotting a rest stop exit, she pulled off and parked the truck. She bought a soda at a vending machine and sat at a picnic bench bordering a little stream. The bubbling water muted the sounds of the freeway traffic. A soft breeze cooled her skin. The cold soda soothed a throat dry from stress and worry. Julie gave a deep sigh as her muscles relaxed.

Perhaps she was upset for nothing. Joe Gordon might never figure out who she was. The note sender might keep quiet. There was a good chance that she would finish the project and return home with her secret intact. As long as that possibility existed, she couldn't justify running away.

Finally, thoroughly refreshed, she returned to her truck and left the rest stop, turning in the direction of Cooperville. As she drove along, she decided that if she were going to stay in Cooperville, the one thing she had better do was cool her budding relationship with Gregory. Even if he never found out her secret, nothing permanent could ever develop between them.

A heavy lump of sadness settled next to Julie's heart. However, that was the truth of the matter, and she'd better learn to accept it.

Chapter Eleven

"Shouldn't that line be a little higher?" Julie asked, pointing to where Audra DeSoto was taping a piece of string to the library wall.

"I'll re-measure." Audra picked up a yardstick and placed it against the wall. "Right. The square is off about an inch. Guess I didn't measure accurately before."

"No problem. An inch isn't much when people will be viewing this from a distance, but if we get too many lines off, it will certainly show." Julie held her end of the string steady while Audra taped hers to the correct spot.

They were using string to make a wall grid that matched the grid Julie had drawn on her sketch of the mural. By transferring the picture from the sketch's grid to the wall's grid, they would be sure to keep the mural accurate. The string would be easy to dispense with when they were finished with it.

Yesterday, the Monday after Millie's dinner party, Julie had helped the newly arrived Audra to settle in with her friend, Beth, who lived in the neighboring town of Barton. It was only a fifteen minute drive away, so Audra would have an easy commute. There was even a picturesque back road she could travel, if she didn't want to cope with freeway traffic.

Julie and Audra met in an art workshop in Seattle two years ago and had quickly become friends. Audra's realistic painting style was similar to hers, which made Audra the logical person to choose as an assistant for the highly detailed wall murals. Audra was twenty-five; however, with her petite build, large, round eyes, and upturned, freckled nose, she looked more like a teenager.

Today, dressed in T-shirt, white overalls, and with her sandy-colored ponytail protruding from the back of her baseball cap, she looked very much the painter.

The piece of string in question now securely fastened, Julie taped another length to her end of the wall. Then she passed the ball of string to Audra, to unwind to her end.

"So you're staying at Millie Linscott's?" Audra cut the string and tossed the ball back to Julie.

"Yes, she practically insisted I move out there, saying it'd be a better place than the inn to do my preliminary work. And she was right. The guestroom is lovely and I have much more room to spread things out. She's really nice, too. You'll meet her. I'm sure she'll be inviting you to dinner soon."

"And the guy who drove you here this morning is her grandson?"

"Uh-huh. Gregory. I'm really just riding with him because Millie suggested it."

"He sure is good-looking. Married? Engaged? In a relationship?"

"None of the above."

"Whew, that's a relief."

Julie's head shot up. "Why? Are you interested?"

Audra flashed a teasing grin. "I might be, if he wasn't so interested in you."

A warm blush spread over Julie's cheeks. "Is it that obvious?"

"Yep. I can tell by the long, soulful look he gave you when he dropped you off. So, do you like him? You'd be crazy not to be interested. You don't have any ties back in Seattle, unless there's something you're not telling me."

"You're right; no permanent ties. The last guy I dated was Frank Morelli, remember him?"

"Oh, yeah. The artist's rep who wanted to take on some of your paintings."

"Right. He was nice enough, but the sparks just never flew. You know what I mean?'

"Definitely. Yah gotta have sparks. So are there any with Gregory? On your part, I mean? We already know there are on his."

"I'm only here in Cooperville temporarily," Julie said, hoping to evade further questions. "There's no point in my getting involved with anyone."

Although Audra was a good friend, Julie did not want to tell her the real reason she could not enter into a relationship with Gregory Linscott. The fewer people who knew her secret the better.

"I'm glad you're available, then," Audra said, "because Beth wants us to go out some Friday night with her group. She told me about a place in Barton that plays country western music and has great barbecue."

"That might be fun." Then, to discourage any more questions about Gregory, Julie quickly added, "We need to put up the scaffolding to do the rest of the grid."

It took them several minutes to unfold and set up the portable scaffolding. Standing on it, they finished taping the grid. The talk centered on their work, but the back of Julie's mind lingered on what Audra had said about Gregory. If Audra so easily observed his interest in her, had others, also? Had Millie? What would she think of her grandson pursuing Julie?

Nora Martindale came around the corner of the building. Holding up her ankle-length, Indian-print skirt, she stepped carefully through the still dewy grass. She stopped below them and gazed up, shading her eyes against the sun peeking over the top of the building. "Good morning, ladies. Looks like you're hard at work. But you're invited to come in for coffee and cake whenever you can take a break. We're celebrating a staff member's birthday."

"That sounds good," Julie said. "As soon as we finish our grid, we'll be in."

An hour later, after enjoying carrot cake and freshly brewed coffee, Julie and Audra emerged from the library. "Guess we'd better get started sketching the picture," Julie said. She walked to her toolbox, opened it, and took out a plastic pouch full of chalk. She handed a piece to Audra.

"I hope it doesn't rain and wash this off," Audra said, brushing flakes of dust from the chalk.

Julie rummaged through the bag, selecting a piece of chalk for herself. "According to the local TV weatherman, it's supposed to be good weather all this week. By that time, we'll have the undercoats in place and the chalk won't matter. But if it washes off, we can always draw it again. Why don't you start at that end, with the sketch of the original building, and I'll work at this end on the picture of the first librarian."

Standing on scaffolding and holding her small sketch in one hand, she drew the picture onto the wall. The sun arced over the building, beating down on them as noon approached.

After a while, she heard a commotion below. She looked down to see the same group of teenagers who'd been there the other day. At least, they appeared to be the same ones. She recognized the two girls with the pink and lime green hair and boy with bleached blond hair and nostril ring, whom she'd spoken to on that other occasion. The one who'd scoffed at the murals project.

Apprehension skittered down Julie's spine. They looked

tough standing there, legs apart, hands on their hips, as though ready to pounce. She shrugged off her troublesome feeling. Surely, she had nothing to fear from these kids. They were just teenagers, for heaven's sake, barely out of childhood.

"Hi," she called cheerfully. "How're you all today?"

Audra turned and smiled at the teenagers. "Hi, guys."

A few of the group mumbled, "Hi," as though it were a real effort to answer.

Julie thought about climbing down, going over to them, and trying to get to know them better. Then she decided against that. Let them watch if they wanted to; that wouldn't hurt anything. She went back to her drawing, conscious of several pairs of eyes on her and Audra.

After about fifteen minutes, the kids apparently became bored and wandered off. She breathed a sigh of relief.

"They look like troublemakers." Audra stopped her work to gaze after them.

Julie shook her head. "Just some of the locals who have nothing better to do than hang around. I don't think they'll do us any harm. But they do pose a problem around town. Gregory is planning to open a teen center for them, which ought to help. It probably won't be ready in time to do us any good, though."

"I thought he worked at the Cooperville Bank?"

"He does. The kids' center is something he's doing on the side."

"So the guy's a philanthropist, too."

"Gregory does seem to be thoughtful and caring of others," Julie agreed wistfully.

"I'm telling yah, you ought to rethink your position regarding him. He's a good catch. I'm surprised he's still running around loose."

"He recently came out of a bad relationship," Julie said. Then, seeing no reason why she couldn't share the details with Audra, she told her about Gregory's experience with the deceptive Marlys Stuart.

"I don't blame him one bit for requiring truth and honesty in a relationship," Audra said emphatically, when she finished the story. "And I don't blame him for being super careful next time around, either. I'll bet that now, he has every woman he's interested in investigated. You got any deep, dark secrets, Julie?" Audra laughed, as though it were a ridiculous idea.

"I, uh, secrets? Why, everyone has a skeleton or two in the closet, don't they?" Julie laughed, too; but hers sounded forced and hollow.

Audra's suggestion gave Julie a new worry. Had Gregory already ordered an investigation of her?

"I drove by the library last evening," Fred Hoskins told Julie the next afternoon. They were at the museum for another meeting of the Murals Committee. Fred sat next to her at the long, rectangular table. He sipped from his mug of coffee. "I saw that the mural is well underway. Looks like a chalk drawing."

"It is exactly that, and we've almost got the sketching done," Julie said. "Next will be the under painting."

Across the table from them, Nora Martindale took a chocolate chip cookie from the plate Abby Hawthorn was passing around. "I saw something you need to change, Julie. Before it's too late."

"Oh? What's that?"

"You've put pansies in front of the original building, but they should be petunias."

"Really? I thought I was being faithful to the picture you

gave me. I don't have it with me, but—"

"As I recall, that picture was a bit blurry," Nora said. "I have Jessie Hart's journal. She was the first librarian, you know."

"I do know," Julie said. "She's part of the mural."

"Well, anyway, in her journal, it says specifically that the flowers were petunias. I'll run off a copy for you."

"Thanks. I'd appreciate that. We do want to be accurate."

"Absolutely," Nora said. "If we aren't as truthful as we can be about the past, we might as well be creating fiction and call it that." She shot Millie a hard look. It was lost on the other woman, though, because she had her head bent over a copy of the agenda she'd just passed out to everyone.

"I think I might have a copy of that picture of the library here," Abby said. "I'd be glad to hunt it up. Do I have time, Millie?"

Millie looked up and gave a dismissive wave of her hand. "You can check that out later. Right now, we need to get the meeting underway."

As the committee discussed financial business, Julie's mind wandered back to earlier that morning. She vividly recalled Gregory's disappointed look when she'd told him she would drive herself into town. Her reason was valid, though, as she needed to pick up some paint from a local store.

She'd been glad of the excuse. It helped to put some badly needed distance between them after what had taken place last Saturday. Spending so much of the day together, and then ending up kissing at his house had sent her into an emotional spin. It made her want more from Gregory, and that was a dangerous wish.

So, she'd driven into town, picked up the paint, and delivered it to the library. Then she'd left Audra to complete the wall drawing while she attended this Murals Committee meeting.

"We need to discuss the bank's mural," Millie said. "I trust we'll reach a decision today. We can't drag this on, because Julie is here only temporarily and she needs to begin work on it. Nora, have you come to your senses and agreed to leave Ben Gabriel out of the picture?"

"No." Nora leaned back in her chair and crossed her arms over her chest. "I can't go along with inaccuracy. If you'd been listening to our conversation about the petunias, you'd know that for sure."

"I was listening," Millie said through tight lips. "But comparing petunias with Ben Gabriel is like trying to compare apples and oranges. Surely, you can see the lack of logic in that?"

Fred snickered, then looked apologetic.

"No," Nora said. "I can't."

Millie sucked in a deep breath, clearly struggling for control.

Millie was a warm and generous person, Julie mused. But there was a tough, stubborn side to her, too. She wouldn't want to be on the outs with the woman.

Millie pursed her lips and turned to Abby. "Have you made up your mind?"

Abby was clutching her stomach, as though it hurt. "I— I'm still not sure. More cookies, anyone?" She lifted the plate and held it out. Everyone declined.

"Fred?" Millie asked.

Fred's double chin folded onto his neck. "Can't decide," he mumbled.

The boldness of the committee members amazed Julie. For all of Millie's apparent power, they were standing up to her. Well, good for them. She wished she could verbally cheer them on, but of course that was out of the question. She could be only a witness to this drama.

"Come, come, come, people!" Millie said. "We've got to get this settled."

No one said anything. Fred sipped his coffee. Abby still clutched her stomach and looked as though she wanted to throw up. Nora stared at the ceiling.

The tension in the room finally became unbearable. Julie just couldn't sit through another argument revolving around her grandfather. "Uh, excuse me, but while you're discussing this, perhaps I could be checking on those flowers? If you'll just tell me where to find that picture." She looked questioningly at Abby.

"Why, yes, there's a big folder on my desk of stuff I've pulled. The photo I'm thinking of might be in there. You know where my office is."

"Right." Julie turned to Millie. "Is that okay with you?"

Millie frowned. "Well, I do like you to be in on our meetings, but go ahead."

Exhaling a sigh of relief, Julie escaped the group. In Abby's office, she spotted the folder, sat down at Abby's desk, and began sifting through it. Angry voices from the other room drifted in to her. They were finally talking about it. Maybe the outburst would have a conclusion and the matter could then be put to rest.

Julie clenched her jaw as their voices continued. The mural problem was her fault. That was irrational, of course, but the feeling persisted, just the same.

When the meeting broke up, Millie came into Abby's office. "What a stubborn group," she said to Julie. "Nobody wants to give an inch. What is wrong with them? If I weren't such a fair person, and so true to the democratic process, I'd exercise some executive authority here and declare the mural to be done my way."

Inwardly, Julie had to smile, because it seemed that was exactly what Millie was doing. Aloud she said, "There's still time to decide. I'm sure it will all work out."

"It will when everyone agrees that I'm right!" Millie said, emphatically.

After Millie left, Abby came in carrying a photo. "Here's the picture of the library when it was first built. I guess it wasn't in that folder, after all." She laid it on the desk.

Julie studied the black and white picture. "It's a little out of focus, but I think Nora's right. Petunias."

Abby absently fingered a button on her cardigan sweater. "Nora's always right. I swear she has a photographic memory. But, in this case, what's the point of such nit picking? Who's going to know besides us? Who's going to care?"

"Well, I do want to be accurate, and it's not too late to change that detail on the mural."

Julie made a copy of the photo on Abby's copy machine. When she was ready to leave, she glanced around for Abby to say goodbye. Not able to spot her, Julie left the museum and headed for the parking lot. Glancing at her truck, she saw that someone was standing on the other side of it, the rider's side. It looked as though the door was open, too. What was going on? Surely, the person wasn't trying to steal the truck. Not in broad daylight.

Julie hurried to the truck. She rounded it and came upon the person from behind. Her jaw dropped when she saw that it was Abby.

"Abby! What's going on?"

Abby whirled around, her face beet red. She raised a hand to her lips. "Oh my, oh my."

"What is it?"

142

Julie's gaze traveled over Abby's shoulder to the interior of the truck. On the seat lay a folded piece of paper. It reminded her of the note that had been slipped underneath her motel room door. Alarm arrowed through her.

"Let me see that," Julie said. Abby jumped aside as Julie grabbed the paper. Heart thudding, she unfolded it and read the message:

I know who you are. But don't worry. I'm a friend.

She gazed up at Abby. "Did you see who left this?"

Abby broke eye contact and stared down at the ground. She twisted her hands together and shifted her feet. "I did," she said in a small voice.

"You saw the person? Well, who was it?"

"No, I did it. I left the note."

"You!" Abby was the last person she had expected to be the mysterious note sender. "Did you slip one under my door at the Mountain View Inn, too?"

Abby nodded.

"But, why?"

Abby put a trembling hand up to her cheek in a gesture of dismay. "I'm sorry, Julie. I didn't mean to scare you. That's why I left the second note. The other one said only that '*I know who you are.*' When I got to thinking about it, I realized that might have frightened you."

"You've got that right!"

"I never meant to do that. So, I thought I'd better leave another one to let you know I'm a friend. That I mean you no harm."

Julie shook her head. "I'm confused."

"I'm sure you must be. Come back inside, and I'll explain. If you're not too mad at me, that is?" She scrubbed at her brow.

"I'm more curious now than anything else. Of course, I

want to know the story behind this."

Once inside the museum, Abby led Julie into her office. She shut the door and waved her into a chair, then sat down at her desk. Abby swiveled the chair around so that she faced her.

"Remember the other day, when I told you I'd been married twice, and that in between there had been someone else, but it hadn't worked out?"

Julie nodded.

"Well," Abby said, "the man in between was your grandfather, Ben Gabriel."

Julie sat back, speechless. The ticking of the clock on Abby's bookshelf sounded suddenly loud in the silence.

Finally, she found her voice. "You and my grandfather? I never would have guessed."

"Nor did anyone else, back then."

"Can you tell me about it?"

Abby nodded. "Yes, you deserve to know what happened." She placed a hand on her stomach, as if to steady herself, and took a deep breath before continuing. "Your grandfather's wife had passed away the year before Cyrus was murdered. Shortly after that, I separated from my husband, Edgar. I hadn't started divorce proceedings yet, but planned to. Ben and I met on a blind date set up by a mutual friend. Although Ben had been much in love with his wife and missed her greatly, the attraction between us was instant and very strong. He was a very handsome man, your grandfather." Abby's eyes glowed with the memory.

"Yes, he was," Julie agreed. "I've seen him in a picture Nora gave me of the original bank staff."

"Yes, I know the one you mean. Well, Ben and I wanted to start seeing each other, but my son, Roger, who was three at the time, presented a problem. I wanted to make sure I got custody of him when Edgar and I divorced. I couldn't take any chances on having my husband use my relationship with Ben as a reason why I should not get custody of Roger."

"That would have been a problem?"

"Oh, yes. Things were different back then than they are now regarding children of a divorce. And adultery, even though the parties were separated at the time, was taken very seriously."

"So you and Ben saw each other secretly," Julie guessed.

"Exactly. It was difficult to keep something like that a secret in a small town like Cooperville, but we managed. We went out of town to places where we didn't think anyone we knew would see us. We felt guilty about what we did, but we did it anyway. Such is the power of love." Abby's lips curved into a sad smile.

"So that was the situation when Cyrus was murdered," Julie said.

"Yes, everything would have been so different if it hadn't been for that!"

Julie let a moment of silence slide by. "Do you know anything about Cyrus's murder?"

Abby leaned forward, idly picked up a glass ball paperweight from her desk, and set it on a pile of papers. "Oh, yes, indeed I do."

"Tell me, Abby, please. The murder has been gnawing at me ever since I learned Ben was accused of it."

"Of course, I'll tell you." Abby settled into her chair again. It squeaked a little as she leaned back. "To begin with, someone was embezzling money from the bank. Cyrus and his partners were keeping it a secret, hoping to confront the thief and settle the matter themselves. They feared reporting it to the police would result in bad publicity for the bank. They hadn't been in business very long and were still building their reputation."

"Okay, I got that much from Gregory."

"Anyway, Cyrus decided Ben was the culprit. I never knew why, but I guess as their accountant, he was the logical one. Cyrus asked Ben to meet him in his office one evening after hours. Ben had no idea what Cyrus wanted to see him about, but, of course, when the boss summons you, you go."

"Ben told you all this afterwards," Julie interjected.

"Well, not exactly. You'll see in a minute what I mean. When Ben went to the meeting, Cyrus accused him of stealing the money. Ben denied it, of course. He had not stolen any money. They got into a fight. The next morning, Cyrus was found with his skull crushed."

"And Grandfather was accused."

"Yes. The janitor had seen him go into Cyrus's office. He'd hung around long enough to hear them arguing."

"Gregory told me Grandfather's fingerprints were found on the murder weapon—some sort of statue."

Abby nodded. "A bronze horse. All the employees were bonded, so their prints were on file."

"My mother told me Ben said his prints were there because he'd moved the statue earlier that day."

"That is the truth. You see, the statue had been in Ben's office. It was something Millie had got somewhere—she was the one who decorated the offices. She knew Cyrus liked bronze and that's why she chose that particular piece. Cyrus decided he wanted it in his office, so he asked Ben to bring it to him. I was there earlier that day and I saw Ben carry the statue from his office to Cyrus's." She paused to smile. "I remember it so clearly. I was standing in line to cash a check when Ben came out of his office, carrying the statue. He saw me, and winked at me. I can still feel the thrill I always got at the sight of him." Abby hugged her arms.

To Julie, she looked almost like a young girl again. And there was no doubt in her mind that Abby had loved her grandfather. "But there were no witnesses to say that Ben didn't hit Cyrus with the statue."

"Yes," Abby said, sobering. "There was one witness. Me."

"You? But why didn't you tell the authorities?"

Abby held up her hand. "I'll explain. While Ben was meeting with Cyrus that night, I was sitting in Ben's car in the bank's back parking lot. We were going to have a late dinner at one of our favorite restaurants in Wilton. It was a warm night in September. The car windows were open, as was the window to Cyrus's office, near where the car was parked. I could hear them arguing. As their voices got louder, I began to get worried. Then I heard some crashing sounds. Then Ben came running out.

" 'We had a fight and I punched him,' Ben told me. 'He fell down and didn't get up. I'm afraid I killed him.' I said we should go back in and see if that was true, and we did. Cyrus was lying on the floor. There was no injury to his head, for Ben had punched him in the jaw. I knelt down and felt his pulse. 'He's just knocked out,' I told Ben. Just then, Cyrus started to come to. He looked up at Ben and muttered, 'Get out!' So we did."

"He was alive when you and Ben left?" Julie said.

"Very much so. Cyrus was found dead the following morning. When the police questioned the employees, Ben admitted having an argument with Cyrus and hitting him. Then they discovered Ben's fingerprints on the horse, and arrested him."

"But why didn't you come forward and tell what you knew?" It seemed clear to her that Abby's testimony would have exonerated her grandfather.

"I would have, despite the trouble it might have caused me over Roger. But I wanted to talk to Ben about it first. I didn't have the chance. Ben put up bail and was released before I could get in the jail to see him. Then he left town."

"His bail must have been really high if it was a murder charge."

"It was, but Ben had a trust fund left to him by his father, that he was saving for your mother. I guess he used that. I never knew for sure."

"And isn't it unusual for anyone charged with murder to be allowed bail at all?"

"I guess it is," Abby said. "But that's the way it happened. Ben had a really sharp lawyer friend who was going to take his case. This man was no friend of the Linscotts and he believed Ben was innocent. Apparently, this lawyer got the judge to agree to bail."

"Did you know Ben was going to leave town after he was freed?"

"No. Although, looking back on our last phone call, I realize now that he was saying goodbye to me. He took his daughter—your mother—to her maternal aunt's."

"Yes," Julie said. "Aunt Bea."

"He left her there and then he just disappeared."

"You never heard from him?" Dismay filled her. Surely, her grandfather wouldn't leave someone he cared about, as he had apparently cared about Abby.

"Oh, yes," Abby said. "But it wasn't until years later. Your aunt and mother were under surveillance for quite a while. Eventually, interest waned, and the case was shelved. Eleanor grew up, married, and had you. It was after that when he called me. He told me how sorry he was that he had had to leave me. He filled me in on details about his daughter—and you, knowing, of course, that I would never tell anyone."

Julie's voice dropped as she said, "Did you know he passed away a few years ago?"

Abby nodded, her eyes brimming with tears. "He left a letter with a friend, to be mailed to me in the event of his death, so I got the word." A tear slid down her cheek. She pulled a tissue from her cardigan pocket and with a trembling hand wiped it away. Julie's throat choked up, and she felt like crying, too.

"I wish Ben had not run away," Abby finally went on. "But I understood why he did. The Linscotts were, and still are, very powerful in Cooperville. Ben thought that even with a smart lawyer, he would surely be convicted. Then, too, if there was a trial, our relationship would most surely have come to light, and he didn't want that. He didn't want to do anything that might affect my getting custody of Roger. So, his running away was in part to protect me."

"I'm glad he wanted to protect you," Julie said.

"Yes. I was awarded custody of Roger in the divorce. I was very pleased with that, considering I had my son only a few more years."

Julie recalled hearing from Abby earlier about Roger's horseback riding accident, how he'd been in a coma afterward and had finally passed away. "You've had a lot of tragedy," she said.

Abby smiled her sad little smile. "I suppose I've had my share."

"But I still don't know why you sent me that note," Julie prompted.

"Ah, yes, the note." Abby heaved a sigh. "When you first came to Cooperville to be interviewed for the murals project, I realized who you were. Ben had told me about you and your mother, remember? I was torn between wanting you to get the job, so that I could get to know Ben's granddaughter, and fearing that if you did do our murals, someone else might discover your relationship to Ben."

"Like Joe Gordon, for instance. He says I remind him of someone."

"Yes, and he very well may figure out who. I do see a lot of your grandfather in you."

"I realized how much I resemble him when I saw the picture of the original bank staff."

Abby nodded. "And I've seen how uncomfortable you are whenever the subject of your grandfather comes up. Like the argument about the bank mural."

"I knew before I came here that he had been accused of embezzling," Julie said. "But the murder charge was news to me, and quite a shock, I can tell you."

"I can imagine. But I understand why your mother didn't want to burden you with that."

"She didn't want me to think of him as a murderer."

Abby leaned forward and put her hand over Julie's. "I hope you don't think too badly of me for sending you that note. I just wanted you to know that someone in town is on your side. I wanted to come right out and tell you about Ben and me, but I was afraid to. Maybe with the notes, I hoped subconsciously to be discovered. If that was the case, I certainly got my wish today."

"No, I don't think badly of you," Julie reassured the woman. In fact, she felt a close bond with Abby. "Knowing what happened relieves my mind. But, you know, the Linscotts still think Grandfather is a murderer."

Abby nodded. "That's the bad part."

"I wish there was some way we could prove his innocence, even though he's gone now. Was the money ever found?"

"No, it never was, and I don't know how to prove his innocence. I suppose I could come forward and tell what I know, but it's still not proof. And would anyone believe me, after all this time?"

"I wouldn't want you to do that," Julie said. "But haven't you ever wondered who did kill Cyrus?"

"Yes, of course, I've wondered."

"There's still a murderer out there somewhere." A sudden chill swept over her.

"I know. I used to spend sleepless nights worrying about that; but, as time passed, and nothing else happened, I decided the person is probably long gone by now. It could have been anyone, a stranger, even, who saw lights on in the bank and went in to see what he could find."

"Was there any evidence that theft could have been involved?"

Abby nodded. "Cyrus's wallet was missing, as was his wedding ring, and a gold medallion he always wore. So, it could have been a robbery gone wrong. We'll probably never know."

They chatted for a few more minutes, then Julie gathered up her tote and prepared to leave. At the door, she turned and gave Abby a hug. "Thank you, Abby, for sharing your story with me. It has relieved my mind a lot to learn the truth."

"You're welcome," Abby said. "The important thing now is to get your project finished without anyone discovering your real identity."

"You're right. That's the scary part."

Abby's words reminded her that, although she now knew the sender of the mysterious note, she could not let down her guard. There was still the possibility that Joe Gordon—or someone else—would make the connection between her and Ben Gabriel.

"I'll do everything I can to help you," Abby promised.

"I appreciate that. It's good to know someone in Cooperville is on my side."

Chapter Twelve

"Would you like to dance, Julie?"

Julie glanced up into Kirk Johnston's blue eyes. "I can't do anything fancy," she hedged. She nodded at the dance floor where couples were whirling around to a lively western tune played by a six-piece band. She'd let Audra talk her into joining her friend Beth's Friday night party at the Wagon Wheel, a restaurant and dance hall in Barton.

There were eight in the group, an even mix of men and women. Although no one had been paired up, all evening Kirk had been making eye contact with her and flashing his flirtatious grin. Finally, he'd come around to her side of the table and asked her to dance.

"I'll go easy on you," Kirk said. "We'll keep it simple."

Sitting beside her, Audra poked Julie with her elbow and whispered, "Go on, live it up."

"Okay." She tried to put some enthusiasm into her voice, but the truth was she would be just as happy listening to the music as dancing to it.

Kirk took Julie's hand and led them onto the dance floor. The musicians, dressed appropriately in western garb and sitting on a dais decorated with bales of hay and an old wagon, struck up a slow tune. The woman singer stepped to the microphone and began to sing one of those sad, lovelorn tales that were so popular in western music.

Kirk pulled her into his arms. His smooth steps were easy

to follow, and she relaxed. He wasn't bad looking, either. His high cheekbones and close-cropped, blond hair suggested Norwegian ancestry. His rugged build and tanned skin indicated he probably worked out-of-doors.

So far, she had been enjoying the evening. With its wooden plank floors and overhead lights framed with wagon wheels, the establishment provided a quaint, Old West atmosphere. And, as Beth had promised, the food was delicious. Shortly after arriving, they'd all trouped to the buffet table and filled their plates with barbecued ribs, baked beans, coleslaw, and sourdough bread. Dessert was apple pie or chocolate cake. Julie couldn't decide between the two, so she had a little of each.

It was good to get away from her work for a while. And away from the Linscotts, too. Since Abby Hawthorn had made her startling confession, Julie had spent a lot of time thinking about her grandfather, and about Cyrus's murder. However, when she walked into the Wagon Wheel tonight, she left all that outside the door.

The song ended with a mournful wail from the singer, indicating the story she'd been telling had an unhappy outcome. A heavy twang from the two guitarists followed, then a loud chord sequence from the keyboard player. Julie made a move to leave the dance floor, but Kirk kept his arm tightly around her waist.

"Let's see what they play next," he said.

"Okay." Why not? Another dance with Kirk wouldn't hurt her.

Just then, looking over Kirk's shoulder, she noticed the short-skirted cowgirl hostess greeting a newly arrived foursome. Julie did a double take when she realized one of the men was Gregory Linscott.

As usual, the sight of him chased her breath away. The

overhead lights cast intriguing shadows under his cheekbones and along his firm jaw. His dark blue, western style shirt hugged muscular shoulders, and form-fitting jeans spread smoothly over firm hips and thighs. Hand-tooled, leather cowboy boots completed his outfit.

She finally tore her gaze away from Gregory long enough to notice that his blond cousin Helen was one of the women.

The other woman had short, glossy black hair and an extremely pretty face that had already turned the heads of several men standing nearby.

Both women wore colorful print shirts; short, flared skirts; and cowboy boots, outfits in which they managed to look both western and chic at the same time. Julie wondered if, like Helen, the dark-haired woman was a model, also.

The second man appeared in the same age range as Gregory. He, too, was dressed appropriately for the occasion in a button-down style shirt, jeans, and boots. He thumbed back a dark brown Stetson where hair the color of rust peeked out.

Julie remembered that at Millie's dinner party, Helen had said her former college roommate, Daria, was coming to town. She had wanted Gregory to go on a double date and attend a play with her, Daria, and a man named Tom.

She reasoned that this was probably that foursome, and that the three locals were showing Daria a night on the town.

Whatever, Julie wanted to avoid talking to Gregory. Maybe they wouldn't like the place and would leave. But no, the hostess, felt hat bobbing on her shoulders, menus in hand, was leading them across the room, presumably to a table. Julie ducked her head, hoping Gregory wouldn't see her.

"Something wrong?" Kirk inquired.

"Oh, nothing," Julie mumbled. Poor Kirk; she'd all but forgotten him.

The band struck up a new tune, one with a fast beat. "We'll sit this one out," Kirk said. He took her hand and led her from the dance floor.

Although Julie appreciated Kirk's honoring her reluctance to dance to the fast western songs, she was dismayed to see that their path would soon cross that of the other party. The next thing she knew, she was face-to-face with Gregory.

"Julie!" Amber lights glinted in Gregory's brown eyes. His lips curved into the slightly crooked grin that always enchanted her.

Her breath caught in her throat. "Hello, Gregory."

Gregory turned to his cousin. "Look, Helen, here's Julie."

Helen smoothed her silky blond hair back behind one ear and nodded politely to Julie. Behind her, the other couple looked on with interest.

Gregory's gaze landed on Kirk. "Hello, Kirk."

So, the two men knew each other. Well, then, she wouldn't have to introduce them.

Gregory looked from Kirk to Julie and back again. His smile faded. "You're here . . . together?"

"We're with some others," she said quickly. She nodded in the direction of their table.

Gregory looked across the room. "Why, it's Beth Griswold." He turned to Helen. "You know Beth, don't you?" Helen had barely said yes when Gregory went on, "Look, they're waving us over."

Julie turned to see. Sure enough, Beth and the others were beckoning to them. Oh, no, were they all going to end up sitting together?

"Is there room?" Helen asked in a doubtful tone.

Please don't let there be room, Julie prayed silently.

"We can pull a couple of tables together," said the hostess, who had been patiently waiting while they talked. She way-laid two passing busboys. "Give us a hand moving a table," she told them.

"Great!" Gregory said, and turned to Helen and the others. "Okay with you?"

There were nods and murmurs of agreement all around.

You'll just have to grin and bear it, Julie thought.

Somehow, in the ensuing shuffle of chairs and tables, Julie ended up sitting between Kirk and Gregory. On Gregory's other side was the pretty brunette, who indeed had turned out to be the visiting Daria. And yes, she had done some modeling, too, although just part-time. She was going to graduate school at a university in Oregon, earning her Master's degree in psychology.

When the band took a break, the group engaged in lively conversation. However, Julie's discomfort made it hard for her to relax and join in. The seating arrangement paired her off with Kirk, and she didn't like that. But, then, Gregory and Daria were a couple, weren't they? Julie didn't like that, either.

What was wrong with her? This was just a casual outing. Besides, Gregory couldn't be too involved with Daria, for she had only recently arrived in town. And so what if he was? Julie had no claim on him. In fact, she'd been studiously avoiding him for the past week. She would have avoided him tonight, if it had been at all possible.

". . . And that dog had twelve puppies!" Beth was saying. "Honest, I kid you not." A plump young woman with flaming red hair and an outgoing personality, Beth rolled her expressive green eyes and took another sip of her wine.

"Beth has a million stories, doesn't she?" Kirk said to Julie.

"Yes, it must be interesting to work in a veterinarian's office," she said.

"That reminds me of when I worked on a farm in Oregon," said a bearded man named Matt. He sat next to Audra and had been paying her a lot of attention. Everyone turned toward him as he launched into his story.

When Matt had finished, Kirk leaned close to Julie, stretching his arm across the back of her chair. "Speaking of jobs, I understand you paint murals?"

Julie nodded, and told him about her work in Cooperville.

"Sounds interesting," he said. "Next time I'm over that way, I'll drop around and see what you're doing."

"Still working for Associated Construction?" Gregory interrupted, leaning around Julie and directing his question to Kirk.

Kirk frowned. "Right." He turned back to Julie, opened his mouth to continue their conversation.

"Still out in the field?" Gregory asked before Kirk could get his next remark or question underway.

"No, I have a desk job, but I still get out once in a while to call on clients. A couple of them are in Cooperville, as I was about to tell Julie." He gave Gregory an obvious look that said, "Bug off."

The band started up again with a loud flurry of guitars and keyboard. Gregory ignored Kirk's hint and caught Julie's hand. "Let's dance."

"But I—"

Her beginning protest was in vain, however, for Gregory was already pulling her to her feet. "You don't mind, do you, Johnston?" Gregory asked.

"Go ahead." Kirk sat back, crossing his arms over his chest and looking disgusted.

"I don't do fancy western dancing," Julie said as they reached the dance floor.

"You don't have to. It's a slow one." Gregory drew Julie into his arms.

Being so close to him threw Julie's emotions into a tail-spin. She had felt nothing while dancing to a slow tune with Kirk; but with Gregory she felt everything. The twining of their hands, the firm pressure of his arm around her waist, their bodies moving together in unison, put every nerve ending on alert.

"I was surprised to see you here tonight," Gregory said, drawing back to look into her eyes. "I thought you were too busy to have any fun this summer."

"I came mainly as a favor to Audra. She worries about me working too hard."

"So do I."

"Not to worry," she said lightly. "I'm doing just fine. Everything is progressing on schedule."

"That's good to know."

"How is Daria enjoying her visit?" There, that ought to remind him of why he was here.

"Really well, if right now is a good gauge. Look over there." He nodded across the dance floor. Julie looked and saw Daria dancing with Kirk. They were talking and laughing like old friends. They made quite a contrast, she with her dark hair, and he a blond. Julie sighed with relief. That just might take some pressure off her tonight, as far as Kirk's interest in her was concerned.

But, if Daria took up with Kirk, that would leave Gregory free to be with her. Julie's emotions churned again.

When the song was over and they returned to the table, Daria had moved into Julie's place. "Hope you don't mind?" she said sweetly.

"We discovered a common interest," Kirk said. "Believe it or not, football."

"I watch all the pro games," Daria said. "There's something just so fascinating about the sport."

"That's nice," Julie said. "And no, I don't mind switching seats at all."

"I don't, either," Gregory put in, giving her a look that spoke volumes.

From then on, Gregory monopolized her, leading her to the dance floor several more times. He even convinced her to take a lesson in line dancing with him, led by the band's singer. She was surprised at how easy the steps were, once she got the hang of them.

Later, Julie and Daria happened to be in the Ladies' Room at the same time. The other woman stepped up to the mirror as Julie stood there pulling her brush through her hair, more unruly than usual from all the fast dancing she had done.

Daria opened her small shoulder purse and took out a silver tube of lipstick. She smiled at Julie. "It looks like we did more than just change seats tonight. I hope you don't mind changing partners as well."

"Kirk never was my date," Julie said. "I only met him this evening." She explained how she had joined the group tonight because of her friendship with Audra.

"Well, that's good," Daria said, "because Kirk's going to take me home. Back to Helen's, I mean. I'm staying with her while I'm in town."

Daria tossed her lipstick into her purse, pulled out a comb, and ran it through the glossy black swirl of bangs hanging low over her forehead. Julie watched her enviously. Daria had the kind of hair that stayed in place and looked great all the time. The combing was totally unnecessary.

"That's fine with me," she said to further reassure Daria

that she wasn't moving in on her territory.

"Good luck with Gregory." Daria put her comb away. "He's a nice guy, and as good-looking as they come, but he and I never clicked. Still, Helen keeps hoping. She'd like me to move here from Oregon. We're as close as sisters."

"I heard that you went to college together," Julie said. "But I'm only here for the summer. I'm not looking for a relationship right now." That excuse was beginning to sound like a broken record.

"Poor Gregory," Daria went on, cocking her head this way and that, as she studied herself in the mirror. "He does need someone. He's been such a loner since that thing with Marlys Stuart. Do you know about that?"

Julie gave up on her hair and put her brush away. She moved to one side to allow another woman who'd come in to have access to the mirror. "He told me that Marlys lied about herself and her background."

Daria nodded. "Let me give you some advice. Don't ever tell Gregory a lie. Not even a little white one. He is *sooo* sensitive now."

Julie glanced down and flicked an imaginary piece of lint from her khaki slacks. "Yes, I'm aware of that. But we're just friends."

Daria nodded, as though she were no longer really interested, then said, "See you back at the table." As the door closed behind Daria, Julie sank onto the upholstered bench in front of the mirror. Daria's reminder of Gregory's former relationship with Marlys Stuart threw a damper on her spirits. She'd been having a good time with Gregory and had, for once, forgotten about their problem. Talking to Daria brought it all back to her with a dismal thud.

She reminded herself that the situation had changed, though, now that she knew her grandfather was not a murderer. Now, she needn't feel so guilty around the Linscotts.

Did that mean she could also accept a more personal relationship with Gregory? She thought about that for several moments. Maybe she could go ahead and tell him who she was and what she had found out about Cyrus's murder. Get it all out in the open, once and for all, as she had almost done that day at his house. The day he'd kissed her, the day that had changed everything as far as her feelings for him were concerned.

But that would mean exposing Abby's secret, and she could not do that without Abby's permission. Abby did not want to open up the past and reveal her part in the events of that terrible night. Julie couldn't blame her. Many years had passed, and, although the tragedy had never been forgotten, people had gone on with their lives. Although there still was a murderer somewhere, there had been no more murders involving the Linscotts or their partners. No, Julie did not blame Abby for wanting to keep the past a secret.

Perhaps she could tell Gregory that she knew her grandfather was not the murderer, but not how she knew. That might be a solution. She'd have to think about that for a while, though, to be sure it was the best course of action. Once she revealed her secret, there would be no going back. Julie sighed and idly pushed a strand of hair away from her face. She'd better get back to the party before everyone wondered what had happened to her.

Later, when the evening was over, Gregory said to her, "I'm taking you home."

"But I already have a ride with Audra."

"And Daria's going with Kirk. Besides, I have something to tell you," he said firmly. "You're coming with me, and I won't take no for an answer."

Rather than create a scene, she gave in. She took Audra

aside and explained the situation. "I'm glad," her friend said. "I didn't think Daria was Gregory's type at all."

In the parking lot, with a flurry of "goodbyes," the group climbed into their respective vehicles. No one seemed to notice that she and Gregory had paired off.

What a beautiful summer night it was. Bright moonlight bathed the road in silver and turned the surrounding hay fields into rivers of gold. The mountains were purple ridges outlined against the black sky.

"I've missed your riding into town with me," Gregory said after a few minutes of silence.

"Now that we've started the library mural, there's a lot of running around to do. It works best if I have my own transportation." Actually, she had missed his company, too. She hadn't realized how much until tonight.

"It was fun tonight," he went on. "I'm glad we ran into you." He took his hand from the wheel and placed it momentarily over hers, lying on her lap. "To think we almost missed each other. Helen had her mind set on us going to Pardee's. It's a similar place farther out of town. One of her friends is a member of the band there. I was the one who wanted to stop at the Wagon Wheel. Something told me we should go there tonight. Some kind of ESP, maybe?" He flashed a teasing smile.

"Maybe so. But, whatever, I did have a good time. Everyone here is so friendly. Did you mind that Daria went home with Kirk?" she asked tentatively. She had heard Daria's side of the story, but perhaps Gregory's viewpoint was different.

"Absolutely not! I knew when I first saw you tonight that I would somehow take you home. They just made it easier for me. Daria's a good kid, but we don't have much in common. I know Helen wishes it was different, but it isn't. Never has been, never will be. I just went out with them tonight to get Helen to quit nagging me about it. I probably shouldn't have, though, because I don't want Helen to have any false hopes about Daria and me. But, hey, don't waste your time being jealous." He shot her another grin.

"I'm not!" At that, she thought she'd better change the subject. "How's your teen center coming?"

"Good. I've found a couple of old but usable sofas and chairs, and some people who are moving out of town donated a pool table."

"Have you set an opening date?"

"Not yet, but I'd like it to be before the end of summer. Of course, the center will be open after school starts, but it'd be nice if the kids could be introduced to the idea while they still have so much time on their hands."

They talked some more about Gregory's project and her murals. She enjoyed herself, but underneath lurked a tension that wouldn't let go. She still wondered what he wanted to tell her, and knew her mind wouldn't rest until she found out what it was.

At last, they turned off the main road onto the one leading to Millie's, and in a few moments pulled to a stop in front of her home. Gregory cut the engine. She had by now decided that maybe his "I want to talk to you" was only a ploy to get her to agree to ride home with him. She grabbed the door handle and prepared to get out, a "thanks-for-the-ride" on her lips.

Gregory laid a hand on her arm. "No, don't go yet." He cupped her chin, turned her face to him, and gazed deeply into her eyes. "You look so pretty tonight."

She laughed nervously. He couldn't be serious. "Come on, in my khaki slacks and this old T-shirt? But, then, I didn't bring any western-style clothes with me."

163

"You look beautiful no matter what you're wearing. You're beautiful inside, too."

"Hey, you're making me blush." She was still trying to keep things light, even though the air around them had thickened with tension.

He took his hand away and laid it on her shoulder. "Be serious a minute. Look, I want to tell you something."

"I thought maybe that was just an excuse to get me to ride with you."

He shook his head. "When I saw you with Kirk Johnston tonight, I thought you were out on a date with him. And I didn't like it one bit." He gave a humorless laugh. "And here I was telling you not to be jealous of Daria, when it seems I was guilty of that very thing myself."

"But now you know I wasn't Kirk's date. But even if I were out with him—or with anyone—that shouldn't matter to you."

"It *does* matter," Gregory interrupted emphatically. His eyes darkened with seriousness. "Why can't you see that? Why can't you see what is happening between us? When I danced with you tonight, I felt something special. I feel it every time we're together. I know you do, too. Don't deny it."

"Gregory, please, I don't know if I want to talk about this. It's a dangerous subject."

"Then let's not talk," he said huskily.

Gregory tipped up her chin, and, before she quite knew what was happening, he closed his lips tenderly over hers.

Swept away by a tide of emotion, she responded to his kiss with all her heart and soul by lifting her arms and clasping them around his neck. He slid his arm around her and pulled her closer, as close as he could, anyway, given the Jeep's console between their seats.

Time stood still as she lost herself in Gregory's kiss. It was wonderful, beyond words, even, to be in his arms again, and a realization flashed through her mind. *This is where I belong. This is where I want to stay. Forever.*

Gregory's tongue probed between her lips, seeking entry. There was no hesitation this time, as there had been that day at his house. She opened her mouth eagerly, welcoming the deepening of the kiss. New warmth spread along her limbs, down through the pit of her stomach, deeper and deeper, to her very core.

The kiss went on for long, delicious moments. Julie became quite lost in it, as her awareness of her surroundings faded and her senses knew only Gregory.

He was the first to pull away. But not far, for as he spoke, his warm breath fanned her cheek. "You see," he whispered, running his forefinger along her tingling lips. "There is something special between us. Isn't there?"

"Yes," Julie said solemnly. She gazed into his eyes, heavy-lidded with passion, and with the irises darkened to almost black in the dim light. "There is something between us." No use trying to deny her feelings any longer, either to herself or to Gregory.

He smiled. "Well, well, I finally got you to agree with me."

Filled suddenly with doubts, she bit her lip and glanced away.

"What is it, Julie? What's still bothering you?"

"N-nothing."

"But I know there is. It's like you have some deep, dark secret, or something." He laughed, then sobered. "You don't, do you?"

Tell him, an internal voice commanded.

"I, uh . . ."

The words wouldn't come. She was still caught up in the unexpected turn of tonight's events, in the thrill of being in

Gregory's arms again, of experiencing his deep and passionate kiss. She didn't want to do anything that would risk spoiling this wonderful moment between them.

She *would* tell him the truth, she promised herself, but not tonight. She needed time to plan exactly what she should say. The circumstances, the setting, for her confession needed to be just right.

"I guess everyone has some secrets," she finished lamely.

"Just so they're harmless ones," he said, and kissed her again.

Chapter Thirteen

"Gregory and I went horseback riding yesterday," Julie told Audra over breakfast on Monday morning. They were at Cindy's Cafe, sitting underneath photos from the old *I Love Lucy* TV show. The jukebox in the corner, fed with Audra's quarters—she was a fan of the era's music—played a steady stream of rock and roll. The two women had planned to discuss the murals, but had ended up talking about their respective weekends instead.

"Was it fun?" Audra asked.

"Yes, it was a beautiful day. We took two of his horses and followed the stream that divides Gregory's property from his grandmother's. It goes for several miles."

Julie smiled, remembering how much she had enjoyed being with Gregory. His boyish enthusiasm over sharing a favorite spot had deeply touched her. And the kisses they'd shared while relaxing near the stream after a picnic lunch made her even more sure of her growing feelings for him. Their discussion after the dance Friday night, in which they'd both admitted special feelings for each other, had broken down barriers between them, making it easier to be together.

"You like him, don't you?" Audra said, breaking into her thoughts.

She sighed in resignation. "I do, I admit it. It's fun for now, but there's no future for us."

Audra waved a hand. "Hey, are you a fortuneteller or

something? Besides, don't worry about the future. It'll work itself out. If it's meant to be, it will be."

Julie picked up her coffee cup, savoring the rich aroma before taking a sip. "It sounds like you hit it off with Matt."

"Yeah, he's a nice guy. We discovered we both like to play golf. We made a date to play next weekend, at a course in Barton. I don't know if that interest will carry us very far, though. Depends on if we find some other things in common. If not, like you and Gregory, it will have been fun while it lasted."

Audra shrugged and reached for her second cinnamon bun. Despite her small size, she had a generous appetite and never seemed to gain an ounce.

"I wish I could be as relaxed about relationships as you are," Julie said. But she couldn't, because she knew her feelings for Gregory went far deeper than she wanted to admit.

"Maybe it's not so much being relaxed as it is just being willing to take things as they come," Audra said. "Like I said, what will be, will be. How does that old song by Doris Day go? My mother used to play it on the piano."

"*Que sera, sera.*"

"Right, that's the one."

The talk finally turned to the library's mural and what they planned to accomplish today. "I should be able to start on the background," Audra said. "Do you think we can use the green paint right out of the can for the trees, or should we mix it?"

"It's pretty bright, as I recall," Julie said. "Let's try toning it down with some white."

A few minutes later, she and Audra left the restaurant and drove their respective trucks to the library. They parked next to each other in the lot and walked around to the mural wall.

"We'll take a look at what we need to do," Julie said, "then go to the basement and get our supplies." She stopped short as her gaze landed on the mural. "What on earth?"

The wall and the chalk sketch they had so painstakingly made last week were covered with ugly slashes of black and red paint. Julie felt sick to her stomach. All their hard work destroyed.

"How awful!" Audra exclaimed. "Who would do this?"

They looked at each other and said simultaneously, "The kids."

"We shouldn't jump to conclusions," Julie said. "They might be entirely innocent."

"But they've been hanging around," Audra said. "And looking pretty tough."

She and Audra went into the library and reported the news to Nora Martindale. "How outrageous!" the woman exclaimed. Since the mural wall was on the other side of the library's parking lot, she hadn't seen the damage when she'd come to work. Nor, apparently, had anyone else. Nora reached for her phone. "I'll call the police right away."

Sergeant Malley, a middle-aged man with a pleasant, laid-back manner, soon arrived. He nodded when Julie told him whom they suspected of the vandalism.

"I know the ones," he said, jotting down notes on a clipboard. "They're troublemakers, all right. We'll round 'em up and see what we can find out. If they're responsible, we'll make 'em clean it up."

"As much as I'd like to see them fix what they destroyed, I'm afraid we can't wait for that," Julie said. "We've got to keep on schedule. We'll go ahead and clean the wall ourselves. Besides, that way, it will be done thoroughly and correctly."

Malley cocked a bushy eyebrow at them. "Okay, but is this gonna be a continuing problem?"

"I hope not! When we finish the mural, we'll add a protective coating that will make any future defacing easy to clean off. But I hope you find out who's responsible and give them some kind of punishment."

"We'll do our best," the sergeant said.

After he left, Julie and Audra prepared a solvent solution and cleaned off the graffiti. It was an arduous chore that took hours. They finished later that afternoon and were waiting for the wall to dry when Sergeant Malley returned. He squatted down next to where they sat resting on the grass.

"You were right," he said. "It was that gang of kids that's been hanging around."

Julie's jaw dropped in surprise. "That was fast work. How'd you find out so soon?"

Malley tipped back his hat, revealing a shock of reddish hair. "I got hold of one of their snitches and he spilled the beans. I rounded up a couple more and they confessed. Haven't caught up with the ringleader yet; he's a tough one to locate. Probably hiding out."

She visualized the boy she'd assumed to be the leader, the one with spiky blond hair and the ring in his nose. The one whose lips curled in disdain when she'd told him about the mural.

"You do know his name, though?" she asked.

"Yep. Mike Stanovich."

Audra looked up from a sketch she'd been working on. "What will happen to them?"

"They'll be turned over to juvenile court," Malley said. "Their parents will probably have to pay damages. Maybe they'll have to make some restitution themselves. Community service, something like that. Depends on the judge."

"I hope they're made to take some responsibility," Julie said.

"They have a lot of time on their hands," Audra added. "They need something constructive to do."

The sergeant shrugged. "I agree with you, but I don't have any answers."

That evening over dinner, Julie told Millie what had happened. Millie shook her head. "There's a certain group of kids that have been a big problem in Cooperville for several years. The older they get the worse trouble they get into. I'm sorry your project had to be one of their targets. How far did it set you back?"

"Only a couple of days. The picture will have to be sketched again, of course, but we managed to get the graffiti cleaned off today. Sergeant Malley promised their office would patrol the area more often, especially at night. Still, I'm worried it will happen again."

"If only something could be done about those kids," Millie fretted.

"Gregory's center should help get them off the streets. Too bad it isn't open now."

Millie nodded. "I'm glad Gregory went ahead with his idea. I know he blamed me when the town council voted money for the murals instead of his center. But I don't have as much influence with them as he believes. There were others besides me who wanted our town to have murals. Anyway, from what Gregory's been telling me, he's found some sources on his own."

"Yes, the plans for the center seem to be moving ahead." Julie rubbed her hand across her brow and sank into thought.

"What?" Millie prompted.

"Oh, it's just that I wish there was some way to help those kids learn respect for public property."

"That's apparently something their parents or any other

adults neglected to teach them. Well, I'm sure that someone along the way tried to teach them, but it failed to sink in."

"Maybe. But, when kids get together, peer pressure seems to rule. The graffiti may have been the idea of only one or two, and the rest went along."

The problem remained on Julie's mind all evening. Sleep that night was restless and troubling; but when she awoke the following morning, an idea had popped into her head. It just might work, she told herself excitedly, as she slipped into her shorts and T-shirt.

She would run it by Millie first, then Gregory. Gregory was the most important one to convince, because he would be the most involved. As she headed for the sun porch and breakfast, she saw Gregory seated at the table. Good, she could share her idea with both him and Millie at the same time.

Julie's mind filled with wonder as she recalled how reluctant she had been to eat breakfast with Gregory when she first came to stay at Millie's. Although only a few weeks ago, it seemed like months had passed since then. They had come a long way from that awkward day.

Today she entered the room eager to see Gregory, and not only because of the idea she wanted to share. It always excited her just to be near him.

He glanced up and smiled as she approached. "Good morning," he said warmly, and put aside his newspaper. Since it was a working day, he was dressed as usual in a shirt and tie.

She slipped into her chair. Gregory motioned to the chafing dish of scrambled eggs and the plate of toast in the center of the table. "Breakfast is already here."

"Thanks, I think I'll have my coffee first."

Gregory reached for the carafe and poured her a cup. "I

172

heard what happened to your mural, and I'm really sorry. I know you and Audra put a lot of work into what you'd done so far. It must have really been the pits to discover it'd been vandalized."

The sincerity in Gregory's voice touched her. She was grateful that instead of being hostile, he now supported her endeavors.

"It was," she said. "I could hardly believe it at first. And thank you for your sympathy. Sergeant Malley investigated the case. Did you also hear he caught the culprits? It was the kids who'd been hanging around. The ones we saw that first day when you dropped me off."

Gregory nodded. "No surprise there. It's not the first time they've been on the wrong side of the law."

"I wasn't surprised, either, although I tried to give them the benefit of the doubt. Maybe I should have tried to make friends with them. I thought about it, but never took action."

"It's hard to say. What I'm wondering is, would it have happened if the teen center had been open? I'd like to think it wouldn't, but of course, we don't know." He picked up a piece of toast and took a bite. "What if it happens again?" he asked, after he'd finished chewing. "I can imagine how much time it took you to clean the paint off the wall. Many more times of doing that will really put you behind schedule."

She put down her coffee cup, reached for the spoon in the chafing dish, and ladled the steaming scrambled eggs onto her plate. "I know, and it could happen again. But that's one of the hazards of mural art. It's right out there virtually un-protected, available to anyone who wants to mess with it. There is one good thing we can do, though, but the mural will have to be finished first."

She went on to explain about the protective coating she and Audra would put over the finished mural. While it wouldn't necessarily stop someone from spraying it again, at least subsequent cleanings would be easier.

Millie came in, dressed in a turquoise slacks and shirt outfit that Julie thought looked stunning with her silver hair. She greeted them and sat down in her customary place on the other side of Gregory. He lifted the quilted cozy from the teapot and poured her a cup of tea. The aroma of Earl Grey, along with a curl of steam, wafted into the air.

"I can guess what you're talking about," Millie said grimly. "The library vandalism. It's been on my mind all night. Trying to find a solution kept me tossing and turning."

"Me, too," Julie said. "But I've thought of something that might prevent it from happening again. At least, from the same group of kids. I waited till you arrived, Millie, so that I could tell you both at the same time."

Gregory regarded Julie with interest. "What's your idea?"

She hesitated. Now that she was actually about to share her idea, doubts flooded her. Maybe it wasn't such a good one, after all. Maybe they wouldn't go for it. But they both were looking at her expectantly, and she had to go ahead now.

Gathering her courage, she took a swallow of coffee. "Well, there was a similar instance in Seattle. I wasn't involved in it; I read about it in the newspaper. The situation was basically the same as here; kids kept hanging around where a mural was being painted and eventually they sprayed paint over it. I don't know what kind of punishment they got, if any. The article focused on the fact that a group who specialized in working with teens got them interested in making their own mural."

"You mean they painted a town building's wall?" Millie asked, wrinkling her nose. "But they weren't artists."

"Sorry, Millie," she said, "but I have to disagree with you. Everyone is an artist, in my opinion. Even though a person may not have formally studied the subject, their self-expressions are their art."

"Okay, but then, under your definition, even the graffiti that was sprayed on the library is art," Gregory said.

"Yes, and there actually is a graffiti school of art. But that's not what we want on the Cooperville buildings, especially not when it defaces something else. But let me get back to what happened to the kids in Seattle. The mural they painted was on huge pieces of wood, plywood, I think, that were put together to make a wall.

"When it was finished, there was some discussion about what to do with it. The group behind the project felt that if it were discarded, it would not teach the lesson they wanted to teach. It needed to be used, just as any other mural in the city was. Finally, they decided to attach it to a chain-link fence bordering one of the downtown ferry terminals. Everyone driving by or lining up for the ferry could see and appreciate it. The kids loved the idea and helped to put it up. They had a big reception to inaugurate it, so to speak. The mayor gave a speech and the kids were in the limelight to take credit. It turned out to be a really attractive piece of folk art."

"Are you going to tell us that cured the kids of their graffiti habit?" Gregory mopped up his last bit of egg with a wedge of toast. "If so, I find that hard to believe."

"I don't know firsthand, but, again, to quote the group that sponsored the project, they claimed the kids did develop a sense of pride in their work. And they sure didn't want anyone destroying their mural."

"Sounds like a very successful endeavor," Millie said.

"Yes," she agreed. "And I was thinking we could try the same thing here. The kids' mural could be for their center, either on one of the actual building walls, outside or inside, or on a portable wall, like in Seattle."

"It's an idea," Gregory said. "I might be able to get the building owner's permission to paint a wall—but I sure don't know anything about painting a mural."

"That's where I come in," Julie said. "I'll help you."

He looked at her incredulously. "But you have your own work to do. You're on a schedule."

"I can do both," she assured him. "Especially now that Audra is here." She turned to Millie. "I really think I can help Gregory without sacrificing any time on the project I'm doing for the town."

"There's still the painting on the shed wall that I want you to do for me," Millie reminded her.

"I know, but that wasn't to be done until the other three are finished, anyway. I can stay and do that one."

"True," Millie said. She looked at her grandson. "What do you think, Gregory?"

Gregory's brow wrinkled. "I'm still not sure. There'd be a lot of work to setting it up. We'd have to coordinate with whatever the court's going to do to the kids. This isn't supposed to take the place of punishment, is it?"

"No, it's not," Julie said. "Hopefully, the kids or their parents will have to make restitution for the damage they've done to the library, either monetary or in another way. Sergeant Malley said something about community service. Whatever it is, let them do it. Then we'll start fresh with this project, and make it really fun."

"It could work," Millie said. "But, Julie, are you sure you want to take all this on?"

"I'm sure."

"I'll see what I can set up," Gregory said. "It may take some time, though."

"I've got the rest of the summer."

"I know, but it's going fast. Too fast," he said soberly, favoring her with a look that spoke volumes.

Julie held his gaze for a moment, then shot Millie a glance. Millie grinned. *She knows what's going on between her grandson and me, and she approves.* A surge of elation worked its way up her spine, but she pulled her mind back to the subject at hand.

"There's still plenty of time," she told them. "But I don't want to waste any, either."

Millie finished her breakfast and left to attend to land-scapers who had arrived to install a sprinkler system in her new garden. Gregory reached over and took Julie's hand.

"You're really one special lady, you know that? Why should you care about the kids in our town?"

"I just do."

And I care about you, she wanted to add. But, surely, he knew that already. "The kids deserve another chance. But will you still think I'm special if my idea doesn't work?" she teased.

He gazed deeply into her eyes. "Nothing could ever change the way I think about you."

Julie met his gaze, tremors of excitement coursing down her spine. He sounded so serious, so . . . committed.

Would he still say that if he knew the truth about you? nagged an internal voice.

Impatiently, she told the voice to shut up. She didn't want anything to spoil this happy moment. And, to her utter surprise and delight, the moment was made even happier when Gregory leaned over and kissed her.

From behind the rhododendron bushes at the side of the house, where a workman dug a trench for the sprinkling system, Millie kept one eye on him and the other on the driveway in front of the house. Sure enough, soon Julie and

Gregory came into view, heading toward his Jeep. The Jeep finally had been fixed, and that little incident seemed forgotten. Actually, it wasn't such a little incident, for it had first brought Julie and her grandson together.

They were walking hand-in-hand. Millie smiled. This was quite a change from those first few days. Of course, she'd seen right away that they'd been attracted to each other. But she hadn't said anything to either one. She'd been watching them all along, noting how their relationship had progressed.

The more she got to know Julie, the more she liked her. She liked her professional attitude, and her warmth and friendliness. Her willingness to help the kids raised Millie's opinion another notch. She was such a thoughtful, giving person. Just the kind of woman she would like to have as a granddaughter-in-law.

Julie and Gregory turned to each other and smiled. They looked so happy. She was glad to see Gregory happy, for a change. He'd been so depressed after his experience with Marlys Stuart. Well, Marlys had never been right for Gregory from the start. Seeing him with Julie had convinced her of that.

Millie sighed. She didn't know what the end of the summer would bring. The mural on the shed wall would keep Julie here awhile longer, but after that, what?

Let the two of them figure it out. She'd give them her approval and support. *Now, let love do the rest.* She thought of her beloved Cyrus and her eyes misted. If only he were here to share this happiness with her.

Chapter Fourteen

Julie dug her screwdriver under the lid of the paint can and popped it off. She turned to Gregory, who removed the plastic wraps from a dozen brand new paintbrushes. "Isn't this a luscious color?"

He came over to see. "It's a nice blue, but not as pretty as your eyes." The gleam in his own eyes told her he had kissing on his mind. Sure enough, he leaned down, tipped up her chin, and aimed his mouth toward hers.

She allowed their lips to briefly touch, then drew back. "You'd better cut that out, because the kids will be here soon."

Gregory stood, soberness chasing away his former smile. "We hope."

Julie's enthusiasm waned a little, too. Yes, they could only hope that the kids would show up for this initial session of mural painting at the new teen center. But what if they didn't?

Don't go there.

Gregory returned to preparing the brushes. Julie picked up a stirring stick and began to mix the blue paint. She thought about the past several weeks, the days full of working and planning for this day. Gregory had done most of it. He had thrown himself wholeheartedly into making the project possible. She learned that once Gregory committed himself to something, he gave it his all.

179

The court had ruled that the kids' parents pay for the damages to the library wall. The teens themselves were assigned to work with the town cleanup crew, picking up litter from the streets. That would be an ongoing assignment for the rest of the summer.

Instead of choosing an outside wall for the mural, Julie and Gregory had decided to use one in the center's multipurpose room. The room was quite large and needed lots of decoration. A mural would take care of most of that need. They met with the kids' parents to explain the project. They found that the parents really cared about their children, but had somehow lost control as the kids got older. Peer pressure played a role in how the teens behaved, too; and when one or two of them got an idea, the rest, like sheep, followed along. The parents thought the mural was a great idea.

Julie and Gregory had also decided that the mural painting would be open to any Cooperville teen, not just those who had done the graffiti. Hopefully, this would draw some of the town's better-behaved kids, who could set a good example for the others. It would also provide an opportunity for positive leadership to emerge.

Julie finished stirring the paint and glanced at her wristwatch. Almost ten o'clock, the time they had set for the kids to show up. They had done as much as they could think of to publicize this event. They had arranged for radio announcements and even for one on the local TV channel. They had plastered posters around town. They'd sent letters to other organizations that dealt with teenagers.

"All ready?" she asked.

"Brushes, rags, chalk, paint. Paper and pencils, if anyone wants to do a preliminary sketch." He pointed to where everything was laid out on the canvas-covered worktable. "Let's go over the plan once again, just to make sure we don't work at cross purposes."

Julie added her can of blue paint to the others on the table. "Okay, each kid has his own square to paint." She nodded at the wall, where they had already marked off squared sections. "They can paint anything they want, as long as it has something to do with the town. We'll suggest they paint something they like about Cooperville."

"What if somebody wants to paint something he doesn't like? You know how some kids are. No matter what an adult suggests, they want to do the opposite."

"That's okay, too. Let them express their feelings—but nothing in poor taste."

He quirked an eyebrow. "And who's going to be the judge of that?"

"We will. There have to be some guidelines and rules. Boundaries are what these kids need in their lives. You and I will be painting squares, too, and they will be examples."

"Me?" He pointed a finger at his chest. "I'm no artist."

"Everyone is an artist. Remember, I told you and Millie that."

He grinned wryly. "That's your opinion."

"Just try painting a square, you might like it."

Ten o'clock came and went with no sign of even one teenager. Gregory busied himself readying the center's office for the director he planned to hire. Once he'd obtained the building, the town council had taken a new look at his project. They then authorized the Parks and Recreation Department to set aside funding for personnel to run the center. In addition to a director, there would be two staff members, both trained to work with teens. Gregory himself would volunteer on some evenings and weekends.

Julie had brought her sketchbook today and was working on a problem she and Audra had run into on the theater's mural. They'd finished the library wall last week and moved on to the second of the three proposed murals. The bank's mural still hadn't been decided, but she stopped worrying about it. She had too many other things to claim her attention.

Not the least of which was Gregory. He'd been occupying all of her free time. They'd had several more rides into the foothills, where he'd shown her special places he and his father, Winston, had gone when Winston was alive. They attended a couple of movies at Cooperville's one and only theater, a cozy place that doubled as a stage for the local drama group.

They had dinners at his house, sharing the cooking chores, and also went out to restaurants. On one of their evenings out, they returned to the Wagon Wheel, where, with just a little brushing up, she was able to join him in line dancing again. Sometimes, they just hung out together at Millie's, visiting with her or doing nothing in particular.

She glanced at Gregory now, busy arranging furniture in the office. Warmth encircled her heart. He had become so dear to her.

There had been only one uncomfortable time together, and that was when Gregory took her to visit his great uncle, Harold, in the nursing home.

"Harold is one of the original bank partners, as you know," Gregory reminded her. "I thought you would be interested in meeting him. Besides, I want you to meet all the family."

However, the fact that Harold had known her grandfather made her uncomfortable about visiting him.

Harold's condition also made the visit difficult. The poor man's multiple strokes affected his speech, and he had great difficulty talking. When Gregory told Harold that Julie was the artist who was painting the murals, he frowned and stuttered some unintelligible sounds.

Finally, Harold was able to say, "Th-the b-bank."

"Yes, Uncle Harold, she's painting a picture on the bank, too. Exactly what it will be hasn't been decided yet." Gregory turned away from Harold and mouthed to her, "Should I tell him why?"

No! Julie wanted to shout, but she only shrugged her shoulders instead.

But then Harold grabbed Gregory's arm and said, "W-why?" and Gregory launched into an explanation. "It's because Millie doesn't want Ben Gabriel included in it. Nora Martindale, who's on the Murals Committee, disagrees, and the others, Abby Hawthorn and Fred Hoskins, can't make up their minds. According to Julie, they just go 'round and 'round about it."

"B-Ben . . ." Harold's face turned red and he gasped for breath.

Gregory reached over and laid a hand on the older man's shoulder. "It's okay, Harold," he said over and over, until the man finally calmed down.

The whole scene was terribly upsetting and left her nearly as distraught as the old man was. "I should have known better than to tell him about the controversy," Gregory said later, "but when he asked, I didn't know what else to say. That sure shows you how Ben Gabriel has kept this entire family upset for all these years."

Gregory came out of the office, breaking into Julie's thoughts. "It's ten thirty. How long do you think we should wait to see if anyone shows up?"

"Till noon. That okay?" Gregory nodded. "I'll start painting my square," Julie said. "That way, if anyone looks in, they'll see something going on."

However, as Julie worked on a scene from Cooperville's Central Park, her spirits began to ebb. So far, it looked as though her idea was a big flop.

When noon arrived, Gregory said, "Guess we might as well give up."

Julie dipped her paintbrush in a jar of solvent. "I'm so disappointed."

"At least, we tried."

Just then, she heard the front door open. "Wait, I think someone is coming." She put down her brush and hurried into the outer room.

A boy of about thirteen stood uncertainly by the door, his hand still clutching the doorknob. He had hair the color of straw. A pug nose sat on a pale, freckled face. His outfit consisted of jeans frayed at the hem, a T-shirt that would never see white again, and a faded flannel shirt worn like a jacket.

The boy finally spoke. "This where the painting is goin' on?"

"It sure is," she said.

"Come on in," said Gregory, who'd come up behind Julie.

The teen seemed hesitant. "I just thought I'd see what it's all about."

"Sure. We'll show you," she said. "What's your name?" She and Gregory led the boy into the multi-purpose room.

"Tyler Smythe."

Julie recognized the name. Tyler was one of the teens involved in the graffiti incident, which pleased her. Then she remembered that he was also "the snitch," as Sergeant Malley had called the one who had told on the others.

"Will any of your friends be coming?" she asked.

"Nah, not if I'm here. They're all mad at me for tellin' on them. I gotta pick up trash with them, but other than that, I ain't in with them no more."

"Oh." Julie's heart sank. So the rest wouldn't come if Tyler was here. Great.

However, they couldn't turn Tyler away, either. They'd have to make the best of it.

She and Gregory showed Tyler the mural wall and explained what was to be painted. They assigned him one of the squares. Tyler remained expressionless, hands shoved in his jeans pockets.

"I ain't no artist," he finally said. "I don't even know if I wanna be one. I just came because my dad promised me he'd take me to the baseball game in Wilton if I did."

"Well, I'm glad your dad wanted you to come," Julie said. "And I'm sure you can do better at art than you think you can. But the main thing is to have fun."

Gregory held out a paintbrush to Tyler, while she opened the various cans of paint.

"Here, give it a try and see what you think," Gregory said.

Five minutes later, Tyler was well on his way to painting his square of the mural.

"What is he painting?" Gregory asked in a whisper.

"A kid on a bicycle," she said. "See the wheels? He said he used to have a bike, but it got stolen. That's sad, isn't it?"

He nodded and tilted his head thoughtfully. "That's something I'll put on my want list. Maybe there are some people in town willing to donate old bicycles."

"And the kids could fix them up."

"Yeah." He gave her an admiring look. "You sure have good ideas."

The following day, Tyler returned. To Julie's and Gregory's surprise, he had a boy and a girl with him. Neither of the newcomers had been involved in the graffiti incident. She and Gregory got them all painting.

185

Later, they noticed several kids who'd done the graffiti peeking in the windows. When Gregory went out to invite them in, they ran away. She felt discouraged that their project had not clicked with their target group, but doggedly kept on with the ones who had shown up. They deserved to participate just as much as the others did.

At the end of the first week, Mike Stanovich, the leader of the graffiti sprayers, who sported the spiky haircut and nose ring, ventured inside the center. He stood in the doorway, hands on his hips, and a sneer on his lips.

Julie held her breath. Would he want to join in, or had he come only to make trouble?

"He's the big fish," Gregory whispered to her. "If we can catch him, I bet the others will follow along."

Julie and Gregory wisely kept their approach to Mike low-key and casual. They let him stay where he was, and resumed coaching the others who were painting. Then they asked Mike if he would like to join them. After watching for a while longer, he finally agreed to pick up a brush.

As Gregory predicted, the others soon followed. By the end of the second week, the mural was well underway.

The project was not without its problems. Midway through, two kids got in a fight over who would paint an extra square. One hit the other and before either she or Gregory could intervene, several others joined in. Brushes flew into the air, and paint splattered onto the mural.

It turned out to be a good lesson, though, because when the kids saw what they'd done, they stopped fighting. The damaged squares had to be done over, but the kids dug in and made the repairs. Julie took this as a sign that they were learning to take pride in their work.

At first, the two groups, the one headed by Tyler Smythe and the one led by Mike Stanovich, kept a distance from one another. Gradually, however, the differences between them faded as they joined together in painting the mural.

Several weeks passed and finally the mural was finished. There were twenty-four squares in all, some of the kids having painted more than one. She and Gregory decided to celebrate by treating the kids to a pizza party, catered by a local establishment. They played games of darts and pool and shot baskets on the new court. They'd picked out silly prizes for the various winners. A journalist from *The Cooperville Gazette* came, to write up the story and take pictures.

Everyone seemed to have a good time, and several came up to Julie and Gregory and especially thanked them for creating the center. They promised to come back and bring more of their friends, even after school started in the fall.

When the teens had cleaned up and finally left, Julie studied the mural. The pictures varied from the bicycle scene Tyler had started that first day to scenes of kids playing baseball, football, and basketball. There were pictures of families and pets, and one that centered on someone's schoolteacher. All in all, it was a bright, colorful, and often insightful commentary on the kids' life in Cooperville.

"I think they did a really good job," she said to Gregory. "Only time will tell if it changed any of their attitudes. But, hopefully, it's a start for all the other things that will be going on here at the center."

"It's a great start." Gregory put his arms around her waist and nuzzled her hair. "I can't thank you enough for all you've done."

She shivered with delight at his touch. "I enjoyed doing it."

"I know you did. Me, too. Who'd ever have thought I'd like painting a picture?"

"You did pretty well." She pointed to his square, which

showed the two of them horseback riding through the meadow near his house. "You even got the color of my hair right."

"With some assistance from you, as I recall. But, let's get out of here and go to my house for our own private celebration."

"If you mean food, I'm stuffed with pizza." Julie patted her full stomach.

"Too full for dessert? I have some very good apple pie, and some vanilla ice cream to go on top."

She twisted her head around to look at him. "When did you have time to bake apple pie? I didn't even know you *could* bake. Although I don't know why not; you seem to do everything else."

"Such flattery. No, even though I could take credit, I admit that the pie is from Hilda's kitchen."

"Well, having had Hilda's pies before, *I* admit that's something I can't turn down."

"And here I thought it was my company you wanted."

"Dreamer."

Their banter continued as they turned out the lights and locked the doors to the center. On the ride home, they alternately talked and were silent; to Julie, it was comfortable either way. She gazed out the window at the now familiar landscape as they wound up the hill toward Gregory's house.

Once there, they took slabs of Hilda's apple pie topped with ice cream and mugs of coffee out to the front porch to sit on the swing.

Moonlight filtered through the pine trees and gilded the lawn with silver. The air still held the warmth of the summer day. Somewhere, an owl hooted, while other birds chirped softly. As darkness fell, the yard grew dark and shadows deepened, drawing her and Gregory closer together in the circle of light coming from inside the house.

When they had finished eating, Gregory set their plates on the small wicker table. He laid his arm on the back of the swing and with one foot started them moving. The chain hanging from the ceiling squeaked for the first couple of turns and then was silent. Julie's thoughts turned from the success of the teen center to the man beside her.

When he gently guided her chin around so that he could kiss her, she sighed with delight. A perfect ending to a perfect day. She twisted in the seat, put her arms around his neck, and gave herself wholeheartedly to the kiss. Warmth spread through her. Her heart thudded in her chest, and kept time with his heart beating rapidly, too, as though they were one.

After awhile, Gregory ended the kiss and whispered against her cheek. "Julie, Julie, you must know that I'm crazy about you."

"Crazy is right."

"I'm serious. I'm in love with you."

Love. The very word itself thrilled her. She looked down at her hand lying in his, felt the gentle pressure of his fingers as he stroked her skin. The silence between them grew thick with tension. She knew he was waiting for her to say that she loved him, too.

She looked up and gazed into his eyes, felt herself being drawn into them, helplessly, as though she were drowning. Yes, she loved him. *Oh, yes.* The emotion surged through her with the power of an electrical jolt, thousands of times stronger than the jolts she'd experienced early on when they happened to casually touch each other.

Yet, despite the realization that she returned his feelings, she found herself hesitant to voice them. Every time she opened her mouth to speak, the words choked up in her throat.

"If you're going to tell me I can't love you because you're here only for the summer, or some such thing, save your breath, because I won't accept that," Gregory said. "If two people love each other, there's no problem between them that can't be solved."

Would he still say that if he knew the truth about me?

"Why do you love me, Gregory?"

He smiled. "I heard somewhere that love doesn't ask why; love just is. But if you want reasons, I can think of several. You're beautiful, intelligent, fun, clever. We enjoy each other's company; we work well together. What more could I want?"

After a moment's silence, he added, "And you're honest. That's very important to me, as I've told you."

Honest. If only he knew the truth about that. A sudden wash of shame heated her cheeks and she lowered her gaze.

Gregory tipped up her chin. "I need to know how you feel about me, Julie. Come on, don't be shy."

"I—I love you, too," she barely whispered, looking deeply into his eyes again. *But I don't have the right to—*

He relaxed against her, which emphasized the tension he'd been under while waiting for her to voice her feelings. He smiled, which lifted her spirits, too. But then, as though upon reflection, he wrinkled his brow slightly. "I wish you sounded happier about it. I'm getting the feeling there's something wrong, something that's bothering you."

Julie hesitated as she carefully phrased an answer. "Admitting my feelings for you is a big step for me."

"Is that all?" His smile returned. "Well, it is for anyone. Do you think it didn't take courage for me to tell you?"

"Yes, I see what you mean."

She'd been so focused on her own dilemma that she hadn't thought about Gregory's risk. Putting feelings on the line was hard for anyone to do. There was always the chance of rejection. Since she had rejected him when he first tried to pursue their relationship, she could appreciate that he forged ahead with it, anyway. She was, in fact, mighty glad that he had. She wouldn't have wanted to miss this for anything.

"So, let's not worry about anything else right now." His gaze softened. "One step at a time, as they say."

"Good idea."

Gregory pulled her into his arms. She laid her head against him, felt the steady rise and fall of his chest. He was such a dear man, and she loved him so much.

What about your secret? nagged an internal voice. *When are you going to tell him who you really are and that you're Ben's granddaughter?*

Okay, she *would* tell him about her relationship to Ben Gabriel, as she had promised herself. For several weeks now, she had been thinking about just how and when she would do that.

In mulling it all over, she decided there was something she had to do first, before confiding in him, and she had yet to take care of that.

As soon as that task was accomplished, she would sit down with Gregory and bare her soul. Get the truth out in the open, once and for all. Show him that she was honest, even though it meant risking his wrath and the possibility of losing him.

She imagined the scenario. He would be surprised and undoubtedly shocked. He would be disappointed, perhaps, that she hadn't told him earlier. But then he'd kiss her soundly and assure her that he still loved her, despite her relationship to Ben Gabriel. It wouldn't matter to him what their families had done in the past. Their love was so strong nothing could come between them, certainly not something that had happened so long ago.

Still, as she thought about the scene to come, a flutter of apprehension made her shiver. Did she really know him that well? Was his love for her really that strong and loyal?

The Linscotts were a very strong family, too, and extremely loyal to one another. Gregory had been brought up to hate her grandfather and to believe that he had done his family wrong. Could she go against that and win?

Gregory's voice broke into her thoughts. "You're shivering. Are you cold?"

"A little . . . Gregory, you did say that if we love each other, there's no problem between us that we can't solve?"

He gave her shoulder a reassuring squeeze. "That's right. I firmly believe that."

"Good . . . I'll remember that."

Chapter Fifteen

"I thought there was something going on between you and Gregory," Abby Hawthorn said to Julie.

Julie reached for one of Abby's homemade oatmeal cookies and took a bite. They were sitting on the white, wrought iron chairs in the museum's courtyard, having tea. They met at least once a week since Abby's confession about her relationship with Julie's grandfather. She now considered Abby a good friend and confidante.

"I didn't want to fall in love with him," Julie said. "It just happened."

"That's the thing about love." Abby smoothed back a strand of gray hair disturbed by the light breeze. "Instead of us choosing, love decides for us. That's what happened with me and your grandfather. Neither of us was really looking for someone."

"And when love does choose, sometimes it causes problems," Julie said. "Like it did for you and grandfather, and for me and Gregory."

Glancing at the museum building, she could see Abby's assistants moving about in the main room. In the parking lot, a car stopped to unload a group of elementary school-aged children. Laughing and shouting with typical childish exuberance, they ran toward the entrance.

Today was Children's Day, she remembered, when the museum gave hands-on history lessons and special activities geared toward the younger set. Abby would be leaving soon to help with the program. Julie needed to hurry along here with her own agenda, or she'd have to wait until another time. Another time might be too late.

She took a deep breath. "Anyway, I must tell Gregory the truth about me. I can't go on with the relationship until he knows. But it's not something I can easily do. I wanted to talk it over with you first."

Abby absently fingered the chain on her pink-framed eyeglasses. "What do you think his reaction will be?"

"Gregory says that two people in love can work out any problem that comes between them. So, I'm counting on him forgiving me and going on with our relationship. Oh, I know he'll probably be shocked at first, and angry. But after he cools down, he'll see the matter differently."

Abby's brow furrowed. "You make it sound awfully simple."

"You don't think he'll eventually forgive me?" Her spirits took a dive. She had hoped Abby would share her belief, and thus encourage her to go through with her plan.

"My doubts spring from years of witnessing the Linscotts' hatred for your grandfather. Their feelings run deep. It's not that Gregory doesn't have a mind of his own. From what I've seen of him, he's his own person. But, remember, he had a lifetime of brainwashing regarding your grandfather."

Julie nibbled on her lower lip. "You make a good point. Perhaps I shouldn't tell him, then."

Abby spread her hands in a gesture of denial. "No, I didn't mean that. But working it out might not be as easy as you think—or hope—it will be."

"I won't tell him anything about you," she assured the other woman. "I'll just say that I'm Ben's granddaughter. I'll admit that I came here knowing the Linscotts suspected Ben of embezzling from the bank, but that I knew nothing about him being implicated in Cyrus's murder, until that day at Millie's reception when he told me.

"I'll tell him I then called my mother and she confirmed it. She hadn't told me that part of it because she wanted to protect me, especially because Ben hadn't been brought to trial and proven to be the murderer. Maybe withholding that information wasn't the right thing to do, but she did what she thought was best. That's the truth, and it ought to stand for something, don't you think?"

"I do." Abby nodded her agreement.

"I'll add that since Ben is now dead, his guilt can't be proven one way or another. I don't have to say I know for sure he wasn't the thief or the murderer."

Abby's brow wrinkled in doubt again. "But they've believed all these years that he was the one who killed Cyrus. I don't think they'll be changing their minds about that, just because it was never proven in a court of law."

Julie watched a bee circle a rose blossom. Finally, it landed in the center. Its wings fluttered for a few seconds and it flew off again. She felt like she was going in circles, too, like the bee. "I see what you mean," she said.

Abby straightened and said firmly, "I see only one way to make the Linscotts change their minds. I'll come forward and tell what I know."

Julie shook her head. "No, there's no need for you to reveal *your* secret, after all these years."

"It's true I'd rather not," Abby acknowledged. "But I will if it helps you and Gregory. Your happiness means a lot to me, Julie."

Abby's concern warmed her heart. "I appreciate that, really I do, Abby. But no, please don't do that. I'll tell him only what I'd planned."

195

"Are you sure? You could be getting yourself into a heap of trouble. You could be jeopardizing your murals project. I'd hate to see Millie fire you. That would be awful."

"I realize I'm putting my job and my future here on the line. But I just can't go on like this. The guilt, the tension is too hard on me. I'm going to go ahead with it and hope for the best."

"All right," Abby said solemnly. "I'll hope for the best, too."

Julie waited until Saturday to make her confession to Gregory. In the morning, she and Audra worked on the theater's mural. They were almost finished with it, a series of three vignettes. One showed the building in the late 1800s, when it was an opera house. Fashionably dressed patrons were streaming into the building to see a performance. Another depicted it as a movie theater, with the name of the first movie shown on the marquee. The third was a scene from the lovely interior, which, although the velvet curtains had been replaced many times and the seats reupholstered, still had the original crystal chandeliers and ticket box.

There had been no more incidents of graffiti or other vandalism. In fact, some of the kids had come around asking if they could help. She and Audra put them to work carrying supplies and cleaning brushes.

Around ten, Julie took a break and phoned Gregory at the teen center. He often spent part of his Saturdays there, working with the newly hired staff or interacting with the kids. When he answered the phone, she could hear the sounds of a basketball game in progress. "Sounds like a busy place," she commented.

"It is. We're just shooting baskets now, but we've almost got enough signed up for two teams. Then we can have some real games. But, what's up?"

"I called to see if we could get together this afternoon."

"I was just going to call and suggest the same thing," he said, sounding pleased. "How about one o'clock at Millie's? I promised to drop in on her today. Haven't seen her much all week. We'll stay and visit with her awhile, then go to my house."

The time set, Julie experienced a moment of relief. But, as the morning passed, butterflies of apprehension danced in her stomach. Was she doing the right thing? Would this be the end of her and Gregory's relationship?

"You're sure jumpy," Audra said, after Julie dropped her paintbrush from the scaffolding for the third time.

"Guess I'm just a little tired today." She climbed down to retrieve the brush, picked up a rag, and wiped off the dirt clinging to the wet paint.

"Did Gregory keep you out late last night?" Audra teased as she spread brown paint over the outline of a tree branch.

"That must be it," she said. "By the way, how are you and Matt getting along?"

"Really well. He doesn't get all out of shape when I win at golf. I can't tolerate a guy who's a poor loser. The four of us will have to go on a double date one of these days."

"Yes, that would be fun."

If Gregory and I are still together after today.

At lunchtime, her turkey sandwich from the deli stuck in her throat. Not even sips of her bottled soda could wash it down. Unable to finish, she wrapped the uneaten portion in the plastic wrapper and stuck it back in the bag.

During the drive to Millie's, she tried to think about the mural, the scenery, the bright summer day, anything except what lay ahead. She'd rehearsed so many times what she planned to say that she didn't need to go over it again. Best to keep her mind occupied with something else.

She parked in Millie's circular driveway. A green SUV sat in front of Gregory's white Jeep. The vehicle was familiar, but she couldn't think whose it was. Oh, well, it didn't matter; someone was always popping in and out of Millie's. However, she and Gregory might have to wait until the company left before going over to his house, where she would launch into her confession. She hoped whoever it was wouldn't stay too long.

She let herself in to find Hilda in the vestibule. She gave Julie a wide smile. "Why, hello, Miss Julie. Miss Millie and the others are in the living room. You go on in. I'll be bringing in some cookies I just baked real soon. And some tea. I'll make sure I include that mint and tarragon tea you like so well."

Julie returned the woman's smile. "Thank you, Hilda. I'll look forward to that."

As she headed down the hallway, the smell of roses stationed in vases along the way drifted to her nostrils. Fresh air from an open door or window breezed by, along with the drone of a lawnmower.

The minute she entered the living room, even before she had time to look around and see who all was there, she felt the tension in the air. Something was wrong. Terribly wrong. Her heartbeat skittered.

Millie sat on a small brocade-upholstered sofa. She held some papers in her lap, and her silver-framed reading glasses were perched on her nose.

Across from Millie, a glass-top coffee table between them, Joe Gordon sat on a matching sofa. So, that was Joe's green SUV she'd seen in the driveway. He leaned toward Millie, elbows propped on his knees, the pointed toes of his cowboy boots turned out.

Joe. Was he the reason for the tension?

Her gaze moved to Gregory standing by the marble fireplace, arms folded across his chest. Their eyes met. She gave him a tentative smile. He did not return her smile but only frowned at her. Apprehension spiraled down her spine. This was not looking good at all.

"Hello, everyone." Julie hoped her voice held more confidence than she felt. Maybe she was mistaken about what was going on. Maybe they were discussing bank business, or the business of one of their other interests.

Everyone stared at her, their faces grim. Her apprehension turned into heart-stopping fear. Her first hunch had been correct. Something was wrong. Dreadfully wrong.

They know about me, she thought with a sudden flash of insight.

"Come in, Julie," Millie said. "We've been waiting for you."

She stepped tentatively into the room and felt like the fly stepping into the spider's parlor in the old nursery rhyme. The opening lines flitted through her mind. *"Won't you come into my parlor?" said the spider to the fly/I've the prettiest little parlor that ever you did spy.*

"Sit down, Julie." Millie-spider gestured toward a wing chair.

Her legs shaking, she crossed to the chair. Keeping her back ramrod straight, she perched on its edge.

Just tell them the truth now. Don't wait to for them to say it first.

Julie clenched her jaw to keep silent. There was still a chance, albeit a slim one, that this had to do with something other than her secret.

"Joe has brought us some very distressing news." Millie took off her glasses and tapped the papers on her lap. "About you."

Julie's heart sank, her last hope all but gone. Again, she had the urge to blurt out her story. But she didn't. She glanced at Gregory, hoping for some sign that he was on her side. Their gazes collided. His eyes were full of pain. Julie swallowed hard and tore her glance away. She couldn't bear to see him hurt.

"Joe has discovered that you are Ben Gabriel's granddaughter," Millie said.

There, it was out in the open at last. She actually felt relieved, as though a heavy weight had been lifted from her shoulders. But that was short-lived, as Millie pointed a finger at her. "We are all shocked. But, tell us, is it true?"

"Yes." Julie raised her chin defensively. "I am his granddaughter."

Again, she experienced a sense of relief, along with a wave of strength and courage. She had nothing to be ashamed of, she reminded herself, because she knew the truth. The Linscotts were the ones with the misperception of the matter.

Millie, Joe, and Gregory exchanged glances. Joe lifted his bushy eyebrows in an I-told-you-so look. Millie scowled. Julie held her breath as she looked for Gregory's response. The pain in his eyes had spread over his entire face. All the color had drained from it, too, and he looked a sickly white. Julie felt as though her heart had been squeezed in two.

"I find it hard to believe that you came here ignorant of what your grandfather had done," Millie said.

The sharpness in Millie's tone made Julie forget her newfound strength. Her spirit began to crumble into little pieces. She had the urge to jump up and bolt from the room, to run away from their scowls and accusations. However, she didn't want to make a cowardly retreat without first telling them her side of the story. She owed it not only to herself, but to the memory of her grandfather, as well.

Straightening her spine and drawing herself up, she said calmly, "I admit I knew he was suspected of embezzling money from the bank, but I swear I knew nothing of the murder charge. I found out about it on the night of the reception, when Gregory took me on a tour of the house."

Joe's high forehead wrinkled in disbelief. "Why would you know about one crime and not the other?"

"My mother chose to tell me only the embezzling part. She didn't want me to think of my grandfather as . . . as a murderer. A *suspected* murderer," she quickly amended.

Joe gave a snort, as though he didn't think much of Julie's mother's reasoning.

"Whether you knew about that part of it or not, you deceived us," Millie said. "You violated our trust. You knew how we felt about your grandfather and anyone who is associated with him. How could you do this to us, Julie? I would have expected so much more from you."

"I am truly sorry," Julie said. "My mother tried to dissuade me from taking the murals job, but I insisted. I am so eager to make a name for myself as a muralist, and this was too good an opportunity to let pass by. I didn't know at the time that I would be dealing with the bank's mural, and that the subject of my grandfather would come up time and again. It's been difficult for me, too."

"Why didn't you tell us? Why did you let us believe in you so much?" Millie asked.

"I thought if I told you, you'd fire me from the project."

The silence that followed told her that indeed would have been the case. She turned to Joe. "How did you find out? Was it just a lucky guess?"

He shook his head. "I finally realized it was Ben that you reminded me of. I got out an old photo I have of him and confirmed that you two do resemble each other. That didn't prove anything, though, so I had you investigated. It didn't take long for the man I hired to turn up your relationship to Ben."

Investigated? She was shocked. All this time an investigator had been snooping around her private life? And probably that of her mother, too. Now *she* felt betrayed. How dare he? But to express her feelings would only make matters worse. She swallowed down her indignation.

"Then you probably know about my mother and where she lives."

Joe nodded and absently fingered the ivory ornament on his bolo tie.

"And that my Grandfather Ben is dead."

Joe studied his fingernails. "Yes, that was in the investigator's report."

"But that doesn't change anything," Millie said. "He was still a murderer."

Anger welled up inside her. "My grandfather did not kill Cyrus!" she blurted.

Millie's eyes narrowed as she regarded Julie warily. "You sound awfully sure of yourself. How do you know that?"

Julie had to look away under Millie's intense scrutiny. "I . . . just know, that's all."

"Do you have any proof?" Gregory spoke for the first time since she had entered the room.

She shot him a quick glance, saw the ray of hope in his eyes, and that a little color had returned to his face. Julie wanted more than anything to tell them about Abby's involvement. But, no, she couldn't without consulting her first. Besides, Abby should be the one to tell her story.

"No," she said, lowering her gaze. "But it's the truth."

"Why should we believe you?" Joe challenged. "You've

clearly shown yourself to be untrustworthy."

"I didn't ever lie," she protested. "I simply didn't tell you the whole truth about myself. There's a difference between the two . . . isn't there?"

Julie wasn't sure whether or not she believed that there was. She'd been asking herself that same question from the beginning.

"I don't think so," Millie said. "Once you found out about the murder charge and how we feel about your grandfather, you should have told us. You've betrayed our trust."

Joe nodded in agreement. Julie risked looking at Gregory again. He looked thoughtful, as though he might waver. Maybe there was still hope that he, if not his grandmother and Joe, would understand. Still, he wouldn't meet her gaze now. That was a bad sign.

Millie continued. "In light of that, we can't allow you to remain on the murals project."

"But we have a contract," Julie protested.

"We'll have our lawyers work out a termination arrangement that will be fair to you," Millie said.

Gregory, come to my rescue! she pleaded silently. *Now is the time for you to declare your love for me, to say that it doesn't matter, that you forgive me . . .*

But Gregory remained at his post by the fireplace. When Julie looked at him, he met her gaze for only the briefest moment before glancing away.

A heavy silence settled over the little group. Finally, Millie spoke. "Well, I don't think there's anything more to say. Joe, Gregory, come with me to my office. I'll need your help in drafting papers to terminate Julie. We'll have to consult with our lawyer, of course, but we can get something prepared to show him."

Terminate. It sounded as though she were being sentenced

to death. Well, maybe in a way, she was.

Millie and Joe stood and walked toward the door. Gregory followed them, but at the doorway he stopped and let them go on without him.

Now, she thought. *Now he will say he forgives me.*

Julie jumped up and ran toward him. "Gregory, I'm so sorry."

Gregory put up his hands, a signal for her to keep her distance, and she stopped in her tracks. "Sorry doesn't cut it, Julie."

"Why can't we talk this out?"

"What would be the point? I think everything's been said that needs to be." He put his hands on his hips and shook his head solemnly. "I can't believe it. You always seemed so open and honest. Millie trusted you. She invited you into her home."

"I know, and I appreciated her hospitality."

"I trusted you."

"I know. That's why we need to discuss this. Don't you remember saying that two people in love can solve any problem?"

A look of disbelief crossed his face. "Nothing can repair the violation of trust." He turned on his heel and stalked out.

Somehow, Julie made it upstairs to her room. In a daze, she packed up her drawing supplies, still spread out on the table where she'd been working last night. Millie hadn't formally asked her to leave yet, but why wait? It was sure to happen soon. Besides, after what had just occurred downstairs, the last place she wanted to be was in Millie Linscott's home.

She finished with her drawing materials and started on her clothing. The packing of her few possessions went quickly.

Then she sat down and composed a brief note, saying that she could be reached at the Mountain View Inn. She left the note on her nightstand, took a last look around to make sure she hadn't forgotten anything, then picked up her bags and went downstairs.

She had to pass Millie's office, where the three had retreated to prepare information on her termination to give to their lawyer. The door was slightly ajar and voices drifted out into the hallway. Julie quickly scooted past the door, hoping no one would be looking in that direction and spot her.

By the time she reached the vestibule, the long held-back tears began to spill over and run down her cheeks. Thankfully, Hilda wasn't around to witness her misery. Julie hurried out the front door, climbed into her truck, and drove away.

Early Monday morning, after spending two restless nights in her old room at the Mountain View Inn, Julie received a telephone call from the Linscotts' lawyer. The town of Cooperville, which held the contract for the murals project, would pay her in full for work on the library's and the theater's murals. The library wall was completed, and the theater needed only a few finishing touches. They would allow Audra to do those. There would be no penalty for the uncompleted third mural. Since she had received a part of the total amount when she'd begun the job, she would now get the remainder for the two completed murals.

Julie had to admit that was more than fair. But it was with a heavy heart that she agreed. The lawyer set up an appointment for her to come into his office the following day, to sign the agreement and receive her check.

She met Audra at the theater mural, where they had planned to put finishing touches on the picture. But instead of beginning work, Julie suggested they go to Cindy's Café.

"What's up?" asked a puzzled Audra.

"We've got to talk."

"Uh-oh, this sounds like bad news."

At the cafe, they sat in their favorite booth, under the photos from the *I Love Lucy* TV show. With rock and roll music thrumming in the background, Julie poured out the whole story, except, of course, for Abby Hawthorn's part in it.

"Wow," Audra said, "I had no idea all this was going on."

"I apologize for not filling you in." Julie eyed the Danish pastry she'd ordered, wondering if she had the appetite to eat it. "I guess I've been in denial, hoping that it would all go away and everything would be fine. Obviously, that wasn't the case."

"I'm so disappointed in Gregory for not standing up for you." Audra, whose appetite seemed to survive anything, took another bite of her bear claw and chewed vigorously.

Julie nodded. "That was the hardest to take. But the Linscotts are a tightly knit, loyal bunch. They stick together."

They both sipped their coffee for a moment. "I'm sorry this job wasn't all it promised to be, but I'm hoping they'll want you to do the bank's mural on your own. I didn't think to suggest it at the time, but I'll call Millie—no, make that Abby or one of the other committee members—and tell them to recommend to her that you take over."

"I don't think I would," Audra said stubbornly. She leaned back in the booth and crossed her arms over her chest. "Not after the way they've treated you. You're my friend, after all, and I'm nothing if not loyal to my friends."

"I appreciate that, Audra. Really, I do. But if they offer it to you, please don't turn it down on my account. I'd rather see you carry on than have it go to someone we don't know."

"We'll see. They'll have to ask me first, and maybe beg on hands and knees."

Julie had to smile at the image that brought to mind.

"Are you going back to Seattle right away?" Audra asked.

Julie nodded. "I'm leaving tomorrow, as soon as I sign the termination agreement and receive my check. Oh, and part of that money is yours. Can you wait till I get home and get it deposited before I give you your share?"

"No problem. We weren't going to get the final payment till after we were finished, anyway."

"And you'll finish the theater mural, won't you?"

"Of course. But I'm really sorry it ended this way."

"Me, too. But thanks for being so understanding. Right now, all I want is to get away from here. The sooner I get back home, the sooner I can put my life back together."

Chapter Sixteen

The following day, after her appointment with the Linscotts' lawyer, Julie loaded her truck and checked out of the Mountain View Inn. Ten minutes later, she was on the highway. As she passed a large wooden sign that read *Leaving the Town of Cooperville*, her throat choked up. Yes, she was leaving Cooperville. Forever.

Last night, she had called Abby to tell her what had happened and to say goodbye. "You were right. This was not something the Linscotts could easily forgive, not even Gregory. But I must say I'm relieved that it's out in the open now, even if I did lose my job."

"I can't let this happen to you!" the older woman said. "It's not fair. I'm going to tell what I know."

"Thanks, Abby. But I'm afraid that even if the Linscotts knew your story, it wouldn't make any difference. They would still reject me for not telling them in the beginning who I am. No, keep your secret."

"But, Julie—" Abby offered a few more protestations, but Julie remained firm. Finally, the older woman agreed to keep silent.

Julie and Abby had promised to keep in touch, although at the moment Julie never wanted to hear of Cooperville or any of its inhabitants again.

She had many regrets, but the biggest was getting involved with Gregory. She should have listened to the part of herself that told her from the very beginning that a relationship with him would never work. But she hadn't. And now his rejection cut to her very soul.

The miles rolled by, taking her farther and farther away from Cooperville. Gradually, her thoughts turned to her mother, waiting for her in Seattle.

Well, Mom, now you can really say, "I told you so."

Gregory stood in the doorway of the teen center's multi-purpose room, taking a mental survey. Everything was ready for the center's official opening. A director and staff had been hired, the painting completed, the needed furniture and equipment obtained. He should feel great.

Actually, he felt lousy.

He had been on a giant downer since learning the truth about Julie. Her betrayal left a deep, painful wound that just wouldn't heal. He'd gone over and over it in his mind. How could she deceive him like that? Especially after he'd told her about Marlys Stuart and how *she* had lied to him. It wasn't as though Julie didn't know how he and his family felt about honesty. No, she'd heard their position often enough. Still, she'd kept her awful secret.

His gaze landed on the mural, zeroing in on the square he had painted of him and Julie horseback riding through his grandmother's meadow. That had been a great outing. He had spent the happiest days he'd ever known with her. A deep sense of loss filled him, followed by a wave of anger. How was he ever going to forget Julie with that picture staring at him every time he entered this room? Maybe he should have one of the kids paint something else over it. Yes, that was what he would do.

Gregory slammed out the door and climbed into the Jeep. He slumped behind the wheel and stared unseeingly at the empty parking lot, reliving for probably the hundredth time that day at Gran's.

He'd arrived eager to get the visit with Gran over with so that he and Julie could go to his house for some quality time alone together. But before she arrived, Joe Gordon came with his news that he'd had Julie investigated and discovered that she was Ben Gabriel's granddaughter.

At first, Gregory hadn't believed him. There must be some mistake, he'd insisted. Then Joe had shown him the documentation from the private investigator.

When Julie arrived, Gregory wanted to take her in his arms and beg her to tell him that the investigator's report was wrong. But, to his amazement, she readily admitted her relationship to Ben. Gregory recalled the shock and dismay that filled him, followed by red-hot anger. Why hadn't she told him?

But, if she'd told them early on, his grandmother would've fired her immediately. Then, he would never have had the chance to know Julie, much less to fall in love with her. What was that old saying his grandmother was fond of quoting? *It's better to have loved and lost than never to have loved at all.*

Judging from the pain Gregory felt right now, he didn't agree with that.

At last, Gregory started the Jeep's engine and pulled out of the parking lot. For a while, he drove aimlessly around town, still mulling everything over. Julie had wanted them to talk about it, but, as he'd told her, there was no point in that. A situation was either black or white. You decided which it was, and that was that.

Clearly, there was no question how he felt in this case. Even though he'd never known his Grandfather Cyrus or Ben Gabriel, he grew up feeling the loss of Cyrus's death and hating Ben Gabriel and everyone associated with him. Irrational? Maybe, but that was the way he'd been raised. There was no way he could wash all that away, just like that.

He heard Julie's accusing voice. *But you said that two people in love could work out any problem that came between them.* Had he really said that? Did he believe it? Confusion made his head spin.

What would happen if they did try to talk about it? *Don't be a dope. That's only asking for more grief. Just be done with her. Let her go. You let Marlys Stuart go and you got over her.*

But he hadn't loved Marlys like he loved Julie. Since he'd met Julie and known how deep his feelings could be, he doubted he'd ever loved Marlys at all. Infatuation, maybe, but not love.

So, did he really want to let Julie go? Would talking about it do any good?

You could give it a try.

Gregory argued back and forth with himself as he continued driving. Although he came to no conscious conclusion, he suddenly found himself in front of the Mountain View Inn.

What if he went in and checked to see if Julie were there? He didn't have to actually see her; he'd only find out whether or not she was still registered. That seemed very important to him right now.

He parked the Jeep, jumped out, and hurried into the inn. A young woman employee stood behind the registration counter. At his request, she consulted her computer. "She checked out," the woman reported.

"When?"

The woman studied the computer's screen. "About half an hour ago."

Gregory ran out to his Jeep. Maybe she hadn't left town right away, but had stopped by the theater mural to say goodbye to Audra.

Dare he hope that had been the case? His heart pumped harder with anticipation.

At the theater, Audra stood on a ladder, putting a second coat of blue paint on one of the vignettes. When she did not return his smile, Gregory figured Julie must have told her the whole story, and that she was taking Julie's side. Well, he couldn't blame her for that. He just hoped she wasn't too angry with him to answer his questions.

"I'm looking for Julie," he told her.

"Why?" Audra asked warily.

"I want to talk to her."

"Isn't it a little late for that?"

"I don't know. I hope not."

Audra turned away to brush paint on a woman opera-goer's dress. He watched her hand move across the image, slowly and painstakingly. "Come on, Audra, I know you're angry with me. But if you want to help make the situation better, just tell me where she is."

"Don't you think she's hurting enough?"

Gregory heaved an impatient sigh. "Yes, but I'm not in such great shape myself. And I'm not going to hurt her any more. I promise. I only want to fix things between us—if I can."

When Audra turned back to him, he saw the hint of a smile on her face. Yes! He'd gotten through to her at last.

"Well, she *was* here," Audra said. "But she left."

"Okay, then, where was she headed?"

"Why, home to Seattle, of course." She gave him a look that said he ought to know that.

His stomach lurched. Julie had left town already. He'd been afraid of that. After checking out of her room, that was the logical next step, wasn't it? "How long ago did she leave?"

Audra pushed back the sleeve of her paint-spattered shirt

to consult her wristwatch. "About fifteen minutes ago."

Only fifteen minutes. If he was lucky, he could catch up with her.

"Thanks, Audra."

"You'd better keep your promise!"

"Don't worry, I will!"

Gregory ran to his Jeep and jumped behind the wheel. Five minutes later, he was on the highway heading out of town. The jumble of thoughts rolling around in his brain finally had settled into a plan.

Talk. He and Julie would talk.

He hoped talking would bring them back together. He knew now that he wanted her back. He didn't want to give up being with her just because of something that had happened years ago to people he and Julie had nothing to do with, really, except that they happened to be relatives. Why should the two of them sacrifice their relationship over the past? Enough sacrifices had already been made.

Once he had his plan in mind, Gregory bawled himself out for taking so long to come to this conclusion. He only hoped that he could catch up to Julie and make her listen to him. With that in mind, he pressed his foot harder on the gas pedal.

The miles rolled by. The *Leaving the Town of Cooperville* sign came and went. Gregory kept his gaze glued to the road ahead, looking for any sign of Julie's red truck.

More miles slipped by with no luck. There were many trucks on the road, and a fair number of red ones, but none were Julie's. He gripped the wheel in frustration. He had to find her.

His cell phone, lying on the seat beside him, shrilled loudly. He picked it up and punched the talk button. "Hello."

"Gregory? Is that you? I called you at home, but there was no answer. Thank God, you have your cell phone with you."

"Gran, what's wrong?" Her frantic tone sent an alarm harrowing through him.

"It's Harold. He's had another stroke. A really bad one this time. He hasn't been able to pull out of it and is failing fast. The doctor says it is only a matter of hours now."

"Oh, no! I was hoping he wouldn't have any more strokes." It had been several years since Harold's last episode, the one that put him in the nursing home.

"So were all of us. But we didn't get our wish. Besides the stroke, they've discovered his liver and kidneys aren't working well. It just seems his whole body is shutting down."

"This is terrible!"

"I know, dear. But the doctor says we'd better go to the nursing home right away to say our last goodbyes. Violet's there already, and so is Helen. Joe Gordon is going to take me over there now."

"I see." His heart sank. He would have to give up his search for Julie. Uncle Harold needed him. The family needed him.

"There is one strange thing," his grandmother went on. "He keeps asking to see Julie. Can you imagine that?"

Gregory jolted with surprise. "Julie? Why?"

"He won't . . . or can't say. But he's most insistent about it. He got very agitated when Violet told him what we had found out about Julie and that she was going to leave town. I suppose she has gone by now."

"Actually, she left only a few minutes ago," Gregory said. "And it just so happens I'm out on the highway now, looking for her."

There was a moment of silence on the other end and a

crackle of static as Gregory passed through an area where reception was difficult.

"I guess I'm not surprised about that," his grandmother finally said.

"I'm trying to find her so that we can talk. Which is what she wanted to do in the first place, but I refused."

"Yes, talking might be a good thing. . . . Well, if you find her, bring her to see Harold right away, will you? Otherwise, come as quickly as you can. Time is running out."

"I will be there soon," Gregory promised.

Gregory turned off the phone and put it back on the seat beside him. Why would Harold, when he was about to die, want to see Julie?

It must have to do with Cyrus. Gregory could think of no other reason. Did Harold have knowledge of the murder? What if Julie had been right in saying that her grandfather was not the killer?

Now it was more important than ever to find her, and he pressed resolutely on.

Five more minutes passed without any luck. Discouraged, Gregory considered giving up, turning around, and returning to Cooperville. Harold's serious condition nagged at him. He should be at his great-uncle's side, with the rest of the family.

A roadside rest area came into view. He slowed down and scanned the vehicles, what he could see of them amid the trees shielding the parking lot.

His heart leaped as he glimpsed a red truck. It looked like Julie's, but he couldn't be sure. Should he take a chance and stop? He had only a second or two to make a decision.

He pulled into the exit lane and entered the rest area. If it wasn't her truck, he'd give up looking for her and head back to Cooperville.

The noise of the highway diminished markedly as he

threaded his way through a tree-lined driveway to the parking lot. He cruised by the red truck, looking at the license plate. Julie's! Boy, was he glad he'd taken this chance.

Gregory swung his Jeep into the empty slot beside the truck, leaned forward, and peered into the cab. Empty. He glanced around the grounds. There were lots of people about, sipping coffee or soft drinks, walking their dogs, eating at the picnic tables.

But no Julie.

Unable to contain himself, Gregory scrambled from the Jeep. Keeping one eye on her truck, he searched for her. She had to be here somewhere.

After having no luck in the immediate area, he climbed to the top of a rise and looked down on the other side. There she was, sitting beside a stream, her back against a large maple tree. She was gazing up at the sky, looking wistful. The light breeze picked up strands of her auburn hair and curled them around her face.

If Gregory had had any doubts about coming after Julie, the sight of her completely banished them. He was so glad to see her again, he thought his heart would burst. He ran down the incline.

Julie listened to the soft burble of the stream trickling by. The sound of cars whizzing along the freeway was hardly noticeable here. It was so peaceful.

This was the same rest area where she'd stopped that day weeks ago when she'd almost left Cooperville the first time. That day, she'd turned around and gone back. She should have kept going all the way to Seattle, though, for look where her stay in Cooperville had got her.

She honestly didn't know why she had stopped here again. She turned off almost automatically when the area came into sight. It wasn't because she had a decision to make about whether to stay or to leave, as before. No, she had already decided she was going home, and that was that.

"Julie!"

Startled to hear her name, she twisted around. Her mouth dropped open. Gregory ran down the hill toward her.

Her heart thudded with excitement. It was so good to see him again. But, whatever was he doing here?

He skidded to a stop in front of her. "Am I glad I found you!"

Still dumbfounded, she could only stare at him. However, she couldn't help noticing how handsome he looked, dressed casually in jeans and a blue T-shirt. An intense longing filled her.

Brow furrowed, hands on his hips, he looked down at her. "We need to talk."

Coming to her senses at last, she reached inside to the hardened part of her heart and said, "The last time we saw each other you said there was nothing to talk about. I agree with you. We've nothing to say to each other." She cocked her head and thought a moment. "Unless you're here about the termination contract. Although I don't know why you would be. It all appeared to be just what Millie wanted."

He shook his head. "No, not about that. I want to talk to you about us."

"No, Gregory, there is no 'us.' I'm on my way home now. I'm moving on with my life. I just stopped here to rest for a few minutes."

"Look, there's something else that's come up, and time is important." He glanced at his watch. "We've got to hurry."

"What are you talking about?"

He ran a hand through his hair, leaving strands of it on end. "It's Uncle Harold. Just now, while I was out looking for you, I got a call from my grandmother. He's had another, really bad stroke, and he's dying."

"I'm sorry." Her voice softened. "But I hardly see what that has to do with me."

"I'm not sure, either. But, Gran said he wants to see you. He's very firm about it."

Julie knit her brow in puzzlement. "Why? I hardly know the man. I only visited him once."

"It might have to do with Cyrus's murder. Harold knows you're Ben's granddaughter. Violet told him. She said he got really upset when he heard."

"I don't need any abuse from him," Julie said, "even if he is dying."

"Abuse you from his deathbed?" Gregory scoffed. "I doubt it." He hunkered down beside her. "Please, Julie, if you don't come back for any other reason, come back for this. It may be a chance for us to find out the truth about what happened to Cyrus."

"I thought you Linscotts knew the truth."

"I thought we did, too. But now I'm not so sure. Come on, don't make the same mistake I did by hiding your head in the sand."

Julie stared at the water, glinting in the sunlight. Maybe this was a chance to find out what had really happened to Cyrus.

"All right," she said. "I'll go back to the nursing home."

Gregory smiled with obvious relief. He stood and offered a hand to her. Julie tentatively put her hand in his and allowed him to lift her to her feet. She made a move to start walking, but he pulled her against his chest.

"Julie . . ." His lips brushed her cheek; his warm breath cascaded over her skin. Her insides turned to jelly and her knees buckled.

"I just want you to know," Gregory said, "that no matter how this thing with Harold turns out, I want you back in my life."

"Oh, Gregory!"

"Yes, I do. I was wrong that day at Grandmother's when I said nothing could fix a betrayal of trust. I want to hear more about your side of the story. I believe we *can* work through what happened in the past. Will you give me another chance?"

Julie gazed up at him and saw the tenderness in his eyes. The steel band around her heart melted. "Yes, Gregory; of course, I will."

Chapter Seventeen

Back in Cooperville, Julie struggled to keep up with Gregory as he hurried along the nursing home's hallway. Now that they were actually there, she had second thoughts about coming. Though she truly was sorry about Harold's condition, her return meant being in the same room with the hostile Linscotts, like that awful day at Millie's. She must be crazy to put herself through that again.

There was no time to change her mind, however, for Gregory had followed her closely all the way back to town. He had grabbed her hand and kept a tight hold on it since they both left their respective vehicles in the nursing home's parking lot.

Gregory stopped at a half-open doorway. "Here we are."

Julie nodded. "I remember from when you brought me here before."

She looked at him, knowing her fear was written across her face. He placed a reassuring hand on her arm. "Don't be afraid," he whispered. "I'm with you, and this time, I'm on your side."

Julie mustered a grateful smile, but her uneasiness continued as they stepped across the threshold.

The sadness that hung in the room was so palpable she could feel it wash over her. Violet, her silver head bowed, sat at Harold's bedside. She held his limp hand between both of hers. Helen stood behind Violet, gazing over her grandmother's shoulder at the dying man. Her eyes were red-rimmed, her cheeks tear-stained.

Millie stood on the other side of Harold's bed, shoulders slumped in a sign of defeat. Joe Gordon remained a few paces away, his tall form silhouetted by the window behind him.

They all glanced around as Gregory and Julie entered the room. At the awareness of all those eyes upon her, she stopped just inside the door. No, not this again. Her stomach gave a queasy flip-flop.

Gregory put his arm around her waist. "It's okay," he whispered. "I won't let them hurt you."

Millie left the bedside and approached them. Her brown eyes held none of their old warmth, but neither did she appear hostile.

"I don't know what this is all about, Julie," Millie said. "But we felt we should honor Harold's request to see you. I'm . . . glad you're here." She mustered a wan smile.

Julie caught the hesitancy in her voice. "I'm sorry about Harold."

"Come stand by the bed," Millie said, "and I'll tell him you're here. He was awake awhile ago, but then the nurse came in and gave him a pill. He drifted off, and it may be awhile before he wakes up again."

Julie and Gregory followed Millie to Harold's bed. Violet looked up at Julie. She let go of Harold's hand to pull a handkerchief from her skirt pocket and dab at her wet cheeks. She whispered in a shaky voice, "He wants to speak to you. I don't know why."

Helen nodded a solemn greeting. Her face was as pale as her blond hair. Joe Gordon also gave Julie a perfunctory nod, but did not speak.

Flanked by Millie and Gregory, Julie gazed down at Harold. Limp white hair framed a face that was as gray as the walls of the room. His hands, lying atop the bedspread, were shriveled into wrinkled claws. His breathing came in labored gasps. Her heart constricted. How terrible it must be to die like this, in such pain and suffering.

Millie leaned down and spoke into Harold's ear. "Harold, Julie Foster is here. You asked to see her, remember?"

Harold's veined eyelids fluttered open, focused unseeingly on Millie, then closed again.

"He's under a lot of medication," Violet said.

"He hasn't spoken to us since he asked to see you," Helen volunteered. "And that was about an hour ago."

"Give him time," Joe put in. "He's got some strength left yet."

They waited, but Harold did not stir. "Maybe what we all need is a cup of coffee," Millie suggested.

"That would be nice." Helen sank into a nearby straight chair. She removed one high-heeled shoe and rubbed where it had made a red mark on her foot.

"There's some in the visitors' waiting room," Violet said. "I should know. I've been there often enough."

Millie turned to Gregory. "Would you get us some, please?"

Gregory nodded.

"I'll help," Julie said. Despite the truce that had been called for the occasion, she did not want to be left alone with the others.

"You'd better stay here," Millie said, "in case Harold wakes up."

Julie hovered near the door during Gregory's absence, ready to bolt if anyone took advantage of her while he was gone. Fortunately, though, he quickly returned, carrying their coffee on a plastic tray. Everyone took a cup and sipped in silence.

Harold remained asleep.

Julie wandered to the window and gazed at the nursing home's pleasant courtyard garden. Several patients and their visitors were clustered around the tulip-shaped fountain. A trellised arbor led to colorful flowerbeds of roses, marigolds, and geraniums.

Millie came to stand beside her. "I've been doing a lot of thinking about what happened at my house that day," the older woman said. "And, well, I'd like to apologize."

Millie's startling statement rendered Julie speechless. She certainly hadn't expected an apology, but the sincerity in Millie's voice left no doubt that that was indeed what it was.

"Thank you, Millie," she said when she'd recovered her voice. "I'd like to apologize, too. I was in the wrong for not telling you about myself before I agreed to do the murals."

Millie shook her head. "I'm not so sure I wouldn't have done the same thing, had I been in your position. I can well understand your reasoning that your performance on the job had nothing to do with what your grandfather did or did not do. You're absolutely right about that. You were doing superb work on the murals."

"I was hoping you'd see it that way, once you did find out. I was planning to tell Gregory about myself that very same day. I honestly was. I had called him earlier at the teen center and asked him if we could get together. He suggested we meet at your house and go over to his place. I was going to tell him when we were alone."

Millie nodded. "I believe you. And we should have let you have more of your say when we had the confrontation at my house. But no, I charged ahead in my typical bulldozer style." She took a sip of her coffee. "I hope you can understand at least a little about where I was coming from. I loved Cyrus so much, and his death was such a tragedy. And when your

223

grandfather ran away, we thought he must be guilty of both the theft and the murder. Why else would he run if he wasn't guilty?"

"My mother thought he might have been afraid that he would have no chance against your powerful family," Julie said. "And, after meeting you all, I tend to agree with her."

Millie grew thoughtful for a moment. "You could be right. I never considered that. It's true that over the years we have run a few people off. People who we perceived did us wrong, or"—she shrugged—"people we just didn't like."

Millie gazed at Julie with sad eyes. "But now, I want to put it all behind us. As I said, I've been doing a lot of thinking. I want you to come back and finish the murals. It's not that I don't like Audra or think she is not capable; it's just that I want *you* to be there, too."

Again, Julie was stunned into silence. "And the committee?" she finally said. "How do they feel about it?"

"Of course, they want you to return. They never wanted you to leave. They just went along with me, as usual!" She gave a wry smile.

"But what about Harold?" Julie nodded in the sick man's direction.

"We're certainly curious about why he wants you here. But perhaps it's nothing more than the wanderings of a poor dying man's mind."

"I don't know if I want to come back to work, with you still believing my grandfather murdered Cyrus," Julie said.

Millie nodded with understanding. "I can't tell you I now believe for certain that he wasn't the one. But I can say that I am open to being shown differently. But we must face the fact that we may never know, one way or the other. The important thing is to put it behind us, once and for all."

Despite what Millie said, Julie still wasn't sure she could

work for the Linscotts again. "I appreciate your change of heart, and I'll think about it."

Millie smiled and laid a hand on Julie's arm. "What more can I ask?"

Just then, Helen cried, "Harold's waking up!"

Julie and Millie put down their coffee cups and rushed to the bedside. Gregory was right behind them. He put his arm around Julie and drew her to him. Grateful for his support, she flashed him a quick smile.

Then she turned back to the man lying in the bed. Her heart thudded against her ribs. Perhaps now she would learn why she had been summoned here.

Millie leaned over and said to Harold, "Harold, can you hear me?"

Harold's eyes were open. He managed a slight nod.

"Julie Foster is here."

"J-Julie?" he said in a raspy voice. His skeletal-thin fingers clutched the bedspread.

Violet leaned forward and put her hand over Harold's. "Easy, darling."

"Yes, Ben Gabriel's granddaughter," Millie said. "You asked for her. Remember?"

"Ben," Harold said, and squeezed his eyes shut. His purplish lips twisted as though he were in pain.

"He's getting upset again," Violet said. "I told you this wasn't a good idea!"

Harold weakly raised a hand and gestured toward Julie. "Julie. Sorry . . . so sorry."

Julie leaned closer to him. "Why are you sorry?"

"B-Ben."

"Yes, my grandfather. What do you want to tell me about him?"

Violet said, sharply, "Don't badger him!"

"She's not, Vi," Millie said. "Please. Harold wants to tell her something. Let him talk. This could be important."

Harold's eyelids drifted down. The others remained perfectly still, waiting. There was virtually no sound in the room, except for Harold's uneven, raspy breathing. So many seconds passed that Julie was about to turn away and give up. But then Harold's eyes opened again.

"Cyrus," he said. "Ben . . ."

Joe Gordon spoke. "Harold, tell us, did Ben murder Cyrus?"

Harold's gaze slid to Joe, then back to Julie. "No."

"Do you know who did murder Cyrus?" Julie asked.

Tension mounted as they waited for Harold's answer.

"I . . . k-killed . . . Cyrus."

A stunned silence settled over the group. Then Violet cried, "No! He doesn't know what he's saying!"

"Of course, he doesn't," Helen echoed. "Granddad couldn't hurt anybody!"

Could it be true? Julie thought wildly. Perhaps, as Millie had earlier suggested, it was just the ramblings of a dying man.

She glanced at the others. Millie's face was stark white, as though she'd seen a ghost. Gregory was shaking his head in a way she couldn't interpret. Joe's mouth gaped as he stared at Harold.

"Harold, you know you didn't kill Cyrus!" Violet said. "Tell us you didn't!"

But Harold only nodded his head. "Yes. I did."

"But how—why—"

Harold raised one hand in a gesture to stop his wife. "It's all . . . written down. . . . See Ralph."

"He's talking about his lawyer, Ralph Summers," Gregory explained.

"No, no, no," Violet kept saying. She covered her face with her hands and began to sob.

Harold stared at Julie. "Sorry," he said, then closed his eyes. A tear slid out and ran down the side of his face, making a zigzag path through well-carved wrinkles.

He's telling the truth, Julie thought. *I just know it!*

Her shoulders sagged. She should feel joy, but all she felt was a profound sadness. The tragedy of Cyrus's death was obviously much more far-reaching than any of the Linscotts had suspected.

How in despair they must be. Their loved one had just confessed to a crime that they had always believed someone else had committed. And, that loved one now lay dying.

Julie couldn't help but feel their anguish. She, above all, knew how it was to be in their place. She grieved for Harold, too. Surely, he had paid a heavy price for carrying around this burden all these years.

And of course, she felt sadness for her grandfather. But for Harold, Ben could have lived a far different and much easier life.

Once it became evident that Harold had lapsed into unconsciousness again, Julie decided she should leave the family alone. She was, after all, still an outsider in this most private of moments. Plus, she had a lot of thinking to do.

When she told Gregory she wanted to leave, he nodded with understanding. "Don't go far, though. Wait for me in the visitors' room. I'll be there shortly. Then, we'll talk."

"Yes," Julie said, "we'll talk."

227

Chapter Eighteen

"Just a few more days and we'll be finished," Julie told Audra. She picked up a brush and dipped it into a can of turquoise paint. "This color is perfect for that bit of sky that shows through the window. If we darken it a little, it'll work for the men's suits, also."

"Great," Audra replied from where she stood on the scaffolding. "I'll be ready to do the sky as soon as I finish the background."

As Julie carried the bucket of paint to where Audra could easily reach it, she reflected on how happy she was to finally be working on the bank's mural. A month had passed since that sad day in Harold's room at the nursing home. The poor man had passed away about an hour after his startling confession.

There had been some very tense times after that. The Linscotts and Joe Gordon had left Harold's side still refusing to believe that he had told the truth about killing Cyrus. Although this distressed Julie, she couldn't blame them. After decades of believing her grandfather was the murderer, it was no wonder they couldn't change their thinking in an instant.

However, as Harold had told them, he had left a written confession with his lawyer, Ralph Summers. After the Linscotts examined it, Gregory showed a copy of it to Julie. In it, Harold confessed to embezzling the money from the bank, to pay off large gambling debts. He planned to pay the money back before the discrepancy was discovered. Unfortunately, that hadn't been the case.

On the night of Cyrus's murder, Harold had driven by the bank and had seen Cyrus's car in the parking lot. He worried that Cyrus might be making after-hours investigations into the embezzlement and would discover that he was the culprit. Harold decided to go in and see just what Cyrus was doing.

He found Cyrus going over the loan records for which Harold was responsible. Cyrus's hair was disheveled and a purple bruise colored his jaw. When Harold asked him what had happened, Cyrus told him about his encounter with Ben Gabriel.

"Ben insists he didn't steal the money," Cyrus said. "We got into an argument and he punched me. Even so, I believe him. In fact, I now know who did take the money."

"Who?" Harold had dared to ask.

"You," was the reply.

To Harold's horror, Cyrus had discovered that Harold had recorded loans in higher amounts than they actually were, skimming the difference for himself.

Harold tried to explain that he had desperately needed the money to pay his gambling debts, and that he planned to pay it back, but Cyrus wouldn't listen. "I'm going to call Joe," Cyrus said, and reached for the phone.

Harold lunged to stop him. The two men struggled. Harold got the upper hand, punching Cyrus until he was groggy. Then Harold knocked Cyrus against the filing cabinet where he hit his head on the sharp metal corner. The impact knocked the brass horse from where it had been sitting atop the cabinet. The sculpture hit Cyrus on the head, smashing his skull and delivering the final blow. Harold panicked and ran from the building. First, though, he removed Cyrus's wallet, ring, and medallion, to make it look like a robbery.

The following day, Cyrus's body was found. The janitor came forward and said he had secretly witnessed the fight between Cyrus and Ben. Ben was arrested. As everyone knew, when Ben was released after posting bail, he left town.

Harold kept working at the bank. He lived with the guilt of what he had done for all the ensuing years, but he never confessed until he lay on his deathbed.

Julie's thoughts turned to Abby Hawthorn, whose secret was still hidden. Now that the truth about the murder was out in the open, there was no need to divulge her affair with Julie's grandfather, or the fact that she, too, was at the bank on that fateful night. Some secrets, it seemed, were destined to remain so forever.

The matter of Harold's confession, however, had to be reported to the authorities, as it now put to rest the mystery of an unsolved murder. The local newspaper, as well as those of the surrounding towns, got wind of it, and for a few days it had been the talk of the area. As scandalous as the story was, it didn't seem as though it would affect the Linscotts' standing in Cooperville.

"Hey, Julie, how are you doing?"

Jolted from her reverie, she turned to see Gregory come around the corner of the building. As always, her heart leapt at the sight of him. He looked very much the banker today, dressed conservatively in a blue pin stripe suit, a white shirt, and a navy tie.

"Just fine," she called, coming to meet him halfway.

They paused to exchange a kiss, which sent tingles all the way down to her toes.

"We have a date for lunch," Gregory said. His arm around Julie's waist, he glanced up at Audra. "Can you hold down the fort while I take this lady to lunch?"

"Sure." Audra grinned down at them from her perch on the scaffolding.

Gregory and Julie started off, but before they reached the street, she drew him aside to stand under the shade of a large maple tree.

"Turn around and look at the mural from here," she said, "and tell me what you think of it, so far."

She followed Gregory's gaze as he scanned the wall. The scene showed the interior of the original bank, with the original staff in various poses.

Her gaze rested on the drawing of her grandfather, Ben Gabriel. He was easy to pick out because of his curly red hair. Under his arm rested one of the gray ledgers in which accountants of that day kept their records. He was smiling and looking proud. Julie's heart swelled with pride, too, now that Grandfather Ben had taken his rightful place with the rest of the staff.

"I think the mural is great," Gregory said. "I'm glad it shows everyone, including Ben and Harold. They all look so happy."

"I believe they were happy when they started out," Julie said. "But since they didn't end up that way, at least this picture preserves—and honors—the time when they were."

He reached out and fingered a lock of her curly hair. "I'm sure glad I caught up with you that day you were leaving town. But I'd have followed you all the way to Seattle if I'd had to. Somehow, you and I were going to get together again. I'm glad, also, that you agreed to finish the mural."

She gazed up at him. Sunlight shining through the maple leaves dappled his dark hair. "Me, too."

"And that you're going to do the one on Millie's shed. But, after that, will I have to drum up some more murals in order to get you to stick around?"

Julie laughed. "Yep, that's just what you'll have to do!"

"I have a better idea." His brown eyes gleamed with amber lights.

"Which is?"

"That you marry me. Then you'll have a good excuse to stay in Cooperville. I was going to wait till we got to the restaurant to propose, but I couldn't resist asking you, now. The opportunity seemed to present itself."

"Marry you?"

"Why are you so surprised? I'll bet you knew my proposal was coming. We've had all those talks you wanted and worked out our communication problems. I've told you I love you. But, I'll tell you again." His voice lowered. "I love you, Julie Foster. More than you'll ever know, and for as long as I live."

"Oh, Gregory . . ."

"You love me, don't you?"

"With all my heart. But do you think it's too soon for that kind of commitment?"

"I do not! I've made up my mind and there's no point in wasting any more time. Do you need more time?"

"No. I won't be changing my mind, that's for sure!"

"Then what's that wrinkled brow for?" He reached to smooth the grooves away. "Are you worried about what will happen to your business if you live here?"

"No, there's no reason why I can't move the base of my operations here. But I still feel uncomfortable around your family. I think Millie has accepted me, because she was already willing to let go of the past. But I don't know about Violet and Helen. Harold's confession was quite a shock to them. And Joe—he's practically family—I don't think he likes me, either."

"It's going to take more time for them to heal," Gregory said. "But I believe that, eventually, they will come to terms with the truth, and realize that holding a grudge against you is not in anyone's best interest."

"I hope you're right."

"As soon as possible, we'll have your mother visit, so that we can get her together with my side of the family."

"I know she's looking forward to that."

"But, remember, whatever happens among the family, we agreed we won't let it come between us. The most important thing is that we love each other and want to be together."

"You're right," Julie said.

"So, what's your answer to my proposal?"

"Yes, I'd be honored to marry you."

"Oh, honey . . ." He took her by the shoulders and leaned her gently against the tree. His lips closed over hers. His kisses were always sweet; but the one that sealed their engagement was the sweetest of all. Julie's heart sang with joy.

"I'm so glad we're going to share our lives," she murmured when the kiss was over.

"Me, too," he said. "And we can start right now by having that lunch I promised you. Then we'll go pick out our rings."

"That will be fun!"

Gregory tucked her hand into the crook of his arm, and together they headed down the street.

About the Author

Linda Hope Lee has written sixteen novels of romance, romantic suspense, and mystery. Other publications include short stories, critical essays, a how-to-write book, and scripts for educational media. She's been a school librarian and a writing teacher.

Also an artist, Lee enjoys working with watercolors, pen and ink, and colored pencils. She collects children's books, games, and anything to do with wirehaired fox terriers. She makes her home in the Pacific Northwest, a setting for many of her stories. Visit her website at www.lindahopelee.com. Lee loves to hear from readers. Email her at linda@lindahopelee.com.